# Calliope
## and the
## Royal Engineers

**Alex McGilvery**

Calliope and the Royal Engineers

Alex McGilvery

Cover Design by A.P. Fuchs

Airship designed and rendered by Paul Potiki,
at www.bookcoverwhisperer.net



ISBN 978-1-989092-08-8

# Chapter 1 - The Gates of Hell

Green water washed over the window on the bridge of the Kestrel. Only the straps fastened to the harness Cal wore kept her on her feet and at the helm. The water receded as the steamship chugged up the next huge wave. At the pinnacle of the watery mountain, Cal caught a glimpse of waves crashing and tangling as far as she could see.

"Hold on," Cal spoke to the sailor strapped into position. She could barely hear herself over the roar of wind and water as she looked to the right. "We'll be hitting the starboard beam."

"Hold on, starboard beam!" Thomas yelled down the ladder. Others would repeat the call to cover the length of the ship.

Cal adjusted the direction of their travel a few degrees to port to aim at a relatively calm stretch ahead. The Kestrel slid down the wave and crashed into the next not quite straight on. She swore the old girl cursed her as it lurched portside. Thomas grunted behind her.

"Status?"

"Okay, Captain, just shaken a bit."

"Tighten your straps. You go down the ladder no one will be able to help you."

"Aye."

The Kestrel crested the next monster and as Cal had hoped they faced a league or two of smaller waves.

"By the numbers, Sailor. The crew can change watch. Double check the dogs on the hatches."

"Number five watch change." Thomas relayed the order.

Cal guided the Kestrel to keep sharp movements to a minimum. The crew knew their work, she needed to give them time to trade over, maybe snatch a hard bread from the galley.

The Gates of Hell lived up to their name. Most ships travelled the extra 200 miles to go around, but the damn fool passengers wanted to experience the Gates. Lord Sifton insisted it was a once in a lifetime opportunity. Life-ending was more like it, but he offered a handsome bonus and the crew agreed to take the risk.

One in five ships never made it out of the Gates. There would be no search; their names would be entered as lost at sea and become another reason ships should avoid the place.

"Two minutes," Cal said.

"Aye, Captain." Bundo had taken Thomas' place at the ladder. He passed the word down the passageway.

"One minute. All hands, hold fast." Cal deliberately relaxed against the straps. The wave coming was a monster.

"Man on deck!" The shout came from the second position. "Hatch open!"

"Ropes, two men holding, one crawls. You have thirty seconds, then get back inside with or without the idiot."

Movement outside caught Cal's attention. Lord Sifton dragged himself along the rail, hand over hand toward the bow. The passengers were supposed to be in their berths, strapped down.

The steamship slammed into the trough between the waves, water washed over the bow, turning the window in front of her almost black. She'd just lost three men to the Gates. Lines and curves jumped into her head showing the path of ship and men in the water. Her hands moved on their own, spinning the wheel hard to port.

"Hold fast!" Cal screamed. Committed now, she would either do the impossible or take the Kestrel to the bottom of the ocean. Instead of climbing the steep slope, the Kestrel turned broadside and heeled so far over the port rail disappeared beneath the water.

"Hold on, hold on." Cal braced herself to stay at the helm while the deck became all but vertical. Screams floated up from the passageway as water crashed through it

"All safe!" The shout was barely audible over the splashing.

She spun the wheel to port and slowly the Kestrel righted herself and rode the wave. With the following swell, the risk of foundering was high.

"We aren't done. Hang on." She hit the bells to tell the engine room to open her full out.

The ship started up the slope in front of her, not as steep as the leading slope. Three-quarters of the way up the wave, Cal spun to starboard. The ship creaked as it passed broadside to the swell, leaning to the right this time. Then they hit the trough just as she came straight to the wave. This time Cal had no chance to plan her route, they'd lost headway and she pushed against the helm as if she could help her ship up the precipice.

The engine thrummed as the bow rose, and Cal's harness cut into her back. She held the wheel with white knuckles. They reached the crest and the bow slammed down; when they hit the bottom of the trough, the water over the window cut off all light.

"God, help us..." Cal whispered from where she hung in her straps, hands locked on the helm. The Kestrel bobbed to the surface and the light returned.

"Strap in, no one move from their station!" Cal returned her focus to guiding the Kestrel through the turbulent waters of the Gates.

***

The Kestrel sailed on a placid ocean. Cal stood on deck in her dress uniform using every ounce of her willpower to not toss Sifton overboard and let him swim home. The crew in their dress white formed two lines, standing at attention. Death never got easier. Cal had seen too many burials at sea. Thomas had secured Lord Sifton first. He didn't get himself strapped in before the ship slammed him down the passageway, snapping his neck.

"Thomas gave himself to the work on this ship. By the nature of the Kestrel as a research vessel, our tasks are more dangerous." *If a certain self-centred Lord obeyed orders, we would have made it clean.* "Thomas made himself indispensable to the scientists who worked aboard the Kestrel. He will be missed. He had a family back in Anglia. Two sons with salt water running through their veins, and a daughter who keeps house in place of their mother who died a few years back of a fever. *We* will be their extended family. They will not be forgotten by this crew, as Thomas will never be forgotten."

Cal nodded and two sailors lifted the board to let the cloth-wrapped body of her deceased crewman slide into the water, chains wrapped around his body to make him sink rapidly into the blue depths. They saluted one last time, then Cal dismissed them.

"I hope we can get back on schedule." Lord Sifton blocked her way into the ship.

"Did you read the contract you signed when you hired the Kestrel?" Cal put her hands behind her back so he couldn't see how close he was to getting decked.

"I pay you to take me where I want to go."

"I suggest you take a closer look." Cal met his insolent gaze with steel. He looked away. "While you may choose destinations and the path we sail, all passengers agree to obey the Captain and crew at all times. You were ordered to remain in your berth. Going out on deck in the Gates put my ship and crew at risk, not to mention you and the other members of your expedition. Your foolishness killed my man."

"I will be sure to send proper recompense to his family." Lord Sifton stepped back as Cal growled at him. "I wanted the full experience of the Gates of Hell. I couldn't get that tied to my bunk. I'm sorry he died, but it was part of his job."

"Lord Sifton, stay out of my sight. If you disobey me or my crew again, I will have you locked in your cabin for the duration of the voyage."

The man's mouth flapped a few times, but even he couldn't brush off Cal's threat. He fled away toward the lab. Cal turned away and walked at a measured pace to her cabin. Not until she'd closed and locked the hatch behind her did she allow the tears to flow. Cal lay on her berth until the storm of grief passed. It wasn't good for discipline for the crew to see their captain crying.

***

They sailed up the coast of Congu, stopping occasionally to allow the scientists to go ashore. To Cal's eyes, they didn't bring much in the way of samples back on board. Lord Sifton and his three cohorts appeared to be more interested in their endless card game and the depletion of the store of brandy they'd brought with them.

After a week of steaming northward, they made a stop at Lusundi. The crew left for shore leave as Cal and Joliu went over every part of the engine room.

"Without the feed hopper," Joliu said. "We'd never have made it. Spent as much time in the air as on the floor. Finding coal of the quality we need for the hopper will be hard."

"Bundo said he has some connections."

"Good thing." Joliu polished an already gleaming spot of the engine.

"Go ashore, I'll take watch. I'm in no mood for carousing."

"Not safe, Captain." Joliu waved at his deep brown features. "My ancestors came from Sombi. They aren't on the best terms with the Congu. I'd rather not be stabbed for something my great-great-grandfather did."

"Okay then." Cal left him in the engine room. One of the crew sat by the gangway.

"Going ashore, Captain?"

"Looks like it."

"You may want to try the White Moby." He pointed down the dock. "Take the third road, it'll be on your starboard hand half a block along. The folks there are honest and they'll keep you safe."

"Thanks, Hank."

Cal checked to be sure she had her coin purse safe, then walked off the Kestrel. She turned and looked back at the old girl as she did every time she disembarked. Then Cal headed off to find the White Moby. Safe sounded good tonight.

The streets around the harbour bustled with wagons carrying freight to and from the ships, as men carried huge bundles on their backs. Women and children wove through the crowd with baskets or bags. Bundo told her vendors would sell direct to the ships, but one needed caution when bargaining. She left it with him. The fever which forced Captain Henrichs ashore also affected the purser. *Maybe Bundo could try the purser's job?* Thinking about what Joliu had said, Cal took a closer look at the people around her. They weren't as dark-skinned as Joliu, and their facial features were finer. Cal had never noticed.

She'd never bothered to notice. Some scientist.

The White Moby interrupted her musings, but she determined to follow through later.

The tavern had a broken harpoon hanging on the wall along with floats and a bit of net. That was the extent of its decoration. The tables looked hard-used and mismatched; the chairs worse, as if someone had used broken chairs to make a whole. Paul sat with a couple of other crewmen, Jorges and Franz. They were new on this trip. The men laughed, waving their tankards and keeping a small crowd mesmerized.

Paul looked up and red ran across his face before he waved her over. Cal shook her head and smiled, then took a table in the corner.

"What will you have, Sir?" The server took another look and flushed red. "I'm sorry, sorry."

"Don't worry about it." Smiling up at the woman, Cal thought of Merica and her babe halfway around the world. "I'd like something different from what I've been eating on board, but not something that will lay me out sick."

"I know the perfect thing. It is chicken crusted with spices and roasted all day."

"Sounds lovely." Cal thought for a moment. "Bring a glass of wine or tankard of ale, whichever is better. After that, I'd like water."

"Yes, Ma'am." The server bobbed her head and disappeared into the kitchen.

Cal's fingers itched. As Captain, she didn't have much time to draw. Maybe if they laid over here for a few days she could break out her satchel full of her sketchbooks and pencils.

"Here, Ma'am." The woman placed a platter in front of Cal which held half a chicken along with some baked roots and brightly-coloured vegetables she couldn't name. "If the spice is too hot, dip bread in the oil and eat it." She pointed out the tiny bowl and a plate with several flatbreads.

As Cal dug in, the skin of the chicken burned fiery hot in her mouth, but the oil quieted it. The flesh of the bird was fall-off-the-bone tender with a unique taste. The roots and vegetables were a good complement. The roots bland, the vegetable sharp and a bit sweet. Before she realized, Cal had emptied the platter and washed the last of the bread down with the final swallow of her ale.

Paul had a new crowd around him. He'd drink free all night telling stories, his voice carrying across the room as he got into his tale.

"We steamed through the Gates of Hell." He shook his head at the disbelieving looks from the listeners. "I know, I know, crazy, right? But this nob wanted to see it for himself. We was strapped in morning to night with maybe a few minutes to do the necessary. Passengers likely regretted it after the first day."

"Don't get many who sail that deathtrap." A white-haired Congu peered skeptically at Paul.

"Wasn't so bad at the start." Paul didn't see or ignored the look. "Rough, but no worse than other storms we'd been through. After a day and half of pounding waves, we sheltered in the lee of this black island. Nothing grew on it." He shuddered.

"Sea Devil's Island." The Congu looked at Paul with respect. "He's the real deal, only people who've seen that place talk about it."

"After the island, it went from rough to insane, as if two hurricanes were battling. Waves came from all directions. Captain strapped herself to the helm and we steamed without stopping through the night." Paul nodded vigorously as if to prove his Captain's mettle. "We hit a patch which was only rough, not we're-going-to-go-down-any-minute rough. So then the nob decided to go out on deck."

"No!" Someone in the crowd of listeners shouted. "Why sail all that way to kill yourself?"

"Oh, he didn't want to kill himself. He's one who figures he's so important, death will make an appointment to see him. The Captain gave us a few seconds to go out with ropes and fetch him in, but a wave struck and washed him overboard."

"You can't mock death," the old Congu said.

"Now here's the part you're not going to believe, but I swear on my mother's grave it's true." Paul waited for the mixed reaction of his listeners to die down. "That wave swept him overboard and almost carried me and my mate with him. Then the Captain spun the ship and put her on her side halfway up this mountain of a wave. We hung on for dear life, sure we'd seen the end. The ship slipped down the wave and picked up the nob as neat as you like. Dropped him right in our arms. We hauled him in and dogged the hatch. Got the nob tied down, though he wasn't happy. The next wave got my mate. Hit the ship and tossed him like a rag doll down the passageway. Broke his neck, poor bloke. Don't think there was a finer sailor than Thomas." Paul took his cap off and paused. Everyone in the crowd followed his example.

Cal would have thought it was showmanship if she hadn't seen the tears on Paul's face as he lifted the board to send Thomas to his final rest. She put her hand over her heart with the rest. When the moment passed, Paul was inundated with a babble of questions, and people pushing drinks at him.

"Quite the tale," a man with rough stubble on his chin, dressed in canvas and leather addressed Cal. He spoke with an undefinable accent. "Vryot Czrmen." He grinned and his blue eyes twinkled. "Most Anglians call me Bri Curzem."

"Cal Shillingsworth." She put out a hand and he shook it firmly. Paul and the others looked halfway to three sheets to the wind, but all three would react to any threat. Besides, Cal didn't get an impression of threat from the man.

"Not old Shillingsworth's daughter? My uncle used to talk about him all the time. I guided for the man any time he came to Harasah."

Cal waved him into the seat across from her. Bri entertained her with stories his uncle told about her father. Not once did the conversation touch on either of their reasons for being in this country. She did finally place his accent. He came from the Kershian Empire.

Bundo looked ready to attack the man by the cart filled with what might have been melons, except they were bright pink. After three days of watching the man bargain, Cal didn't worry about either of their lives.

Cal nodded to Jorges, who stood on the dock at the bottom of the gangway.

"The usual place?" Jorges asked.

"Yes, I'll send a runner if things change." Cal adjusted satchel on her shoulder and then headed toward the market Bri had shown her. Being with someone who was neither a relation, crew member or suitor felt good. She had no doubt he was up to something, but then Lord Sifton, who'd disappeared with two of his team into the interior, had plans of his own.

Cal placed herself in the shade of a rug merchant's tent and took out her sketchbook. They'd come to an agreement. She got shade, and he got a portrait of him and his large family. Apparently, as a wealthy member of his clan, he was expected to have several wives. Cal never saw any of them without a smile on their face.

She drew people at random, paying careful attention to the challenge of getting the dark skin right. The challenge helped her let go of her anger at Sifton. The man honestly couldn't see what he did wrong. Cal vowed that next time, she'd let him drown.

As they had for the last two days, a crowd of children gathered around Cal. The merchant didn't mind as long as they stayed off his rugs. Cal handed out stubs of pencil and scraps of paper. The children giggled as they drew. If their faces were anything to go by, Cal kept a very serious expression while drawing. At least she didn't stick her tongue out anymore... most of the time.

As the shadows moved across the pavement, a few people gathered up the courage to ask her to draw them. Most were content to peer over her shoulder for a time. Cal looked up when her flock of children scrambled away.

"They told me I'd find you here." Lord Sifton looked down his nose at her. "I expected a Captain to be with their ship. We sail at dawn." He turned and stomped away, people dodging out of his path.

Cal sighed and packed up her gear. She fingered a tiny rug hanging from the side of the merchant's tent.

"Very rare," the merchant said. "Silk from the east. Comes from worms they tell me. You want?"

"It is beautiful." Cal tried to figure how much coin she had in her berth. Surely not enough to purchase such a treasure.

"The third prince had it brought in but didn't like the colour. He won't buy it, but no one can buy something the prince ordered. It would be disrespectful to think one was entitled to own a royal carpet."

*Way out of my league.* Cal regretfully turned away.

"Thank you for your hospitality." She bowed to the merchant, then bumped into a man as she left the tent. The man might as well have been a tree for all the effect she had on him. Cal staggered back to fall on a pile of carpets.

"Help the Lady up, Chiza." Another man, in pants and shirt of canary yellow, which had the same sheen as the tiny rug stepped around the tree and frowned. A massive hand reached down to take Cal's. With surprising gentleness, the huge man lifted her feet, then knelt before her, his drab robes contrasting with the bright yellow. "Chiza is waiting for you to punish him for his clumsiness."

"It was my fault," Cal gazed into the man's brown eyes. Was that humour glinting behind his blank expression?

"Nevertheless, as a servant to royalty, he must not collide with anyone, particularly not a person of your stature, Lady Shillingsworth."

Cal stared him in shock.

"My apologies," the man in yellow said, bowing slightly. "I heard a lady captain had come to port from Anglia. The only such woman I could imagine in that role is you. I had the privilege of attending the Royal Society for Science when you brought in the sea serpent's immense tooth. Ever since I have wanted to meet you. But even princes can't barge in to speak to a Lady, especially not one favoured by the Crown Prince of Anglia himself. Imagine my delight at the possibility of meeting you here. The clansman on your ship was kind enough to tell me you were accustomed to spending time in this market. Surrounded by a mob of children I'm told. Sadly, disease has left many young ones fending for themselves. It is a shame to our country. I hoped to offer schooling and shelter, but history has made them distrustful. Perhaps encouraging art will open the door to their hearts."

The big man still knelt in front of Cal, still as a stone.

"Oh get up." Cal slapped his shoulder lightly. The man stood smoothly and gazed at Cal.

"Chiza doesn't feel his punishment is sufficient." The prince shook his head.

"How about this then? Your punishment is that you will aid the next person who asks you for help regardless of their station, or the nature of the task."

Chiza tilted his head slightly, still holding Cal's gaze with his. Then he nodded and bowed deeply to Cal.

"It appears you have impressed him. A most difficult task." The prince in the yellow suit nodded at her.

"Surely, your Highness, he is impressed by royalty."

"He works for royalty; thus he knows we are only human." The prince smiled, and his face lit up. "I have been remiss." The prince bowed to her. "I failed to introduce myself properly. I beg your forgiveness."

"Don't tell me I'm supposed to punish you as well." Cal let the satchel settle to the ground and rolled her shoulder. The prince laughed and Chiza's lips bent into what might have been a smile.

"How delightful. I will accept the same punishment you gave Chiza. It should be fun." He straightened and the blank mask fell over his face. "Lady Shillingsworth, I am Roger Hrona Xanichi, third prince of the Congu nation." He took Cal's hand and kissed it. She'd always been uncomfortable with men kissing her hand, but he made it as natural as a handshake. "Please call me Roger, it is the name I used in Anglia."

"Well, Roger, I'm sorry to say we are to sail tomorrow at dawn. I have work I must do. However, why don't you and Chiza walk me to the Kestrel and I can give you a brief tour?"

"If only I'd heard sooner." Roger heaved a sigh. "Shall we?" He held out his arm in the Anglian fashion. Cal took it as if she weren't dressed in a captain's working uniform. She must look a sparrow next to his canary.

They chatted pleasantly on the way back to the Kestrel. Roger had been sent by his father to get a full Anglian education. He'd only just arrived back in Congu and was trying to fit back in place.

"It is as if I changed shape while away." Roger's hand trembled under hers.

"The point of going was to change. Don't pretend to be who you were, your country needs who you are now."

Roger walked examining the sky as if it held a map to his life.

"I believe you have given me two gifts beyond price. If ever there is something I may do for you, ask and it will be done or I will die trying."

Cal guided him up the gangway and introduced him to the crew. Most nodded politely, but Bundo knelt before the prince in the same way Chiza had knelt before her.

"You left without the King's permission." Roger's voice cut like a knife. "He had no choice but to exile you."

"My prince, to stay would have meant shedding blood I have no desire to shed."

"And if he'd found you in this place?"

"The Captain takes care of her crew."

"Even against the king of this nation?"

"No one boards the Kestrel without my permission. She is my domain and I hold life and death in my hands." Cal didn't know why she butted into what was clearly a private argument. All three men stared at her while she kept her gaze level.

"I believe that is the solution to my problem." Roger relaxed and his voice returned to the bantering tone he'd kept with Cal. "This is Captain Shillingsworth's domain.  I have no power here, but I can't ignore that you returned against the King's edict. Your life belongs to Captain Shillingsworth. Wherever she goes, you will follow.

You will be my hand to protect her." Roger turned to Cal. "Shall we finish the tour?"  He guided her away from the man weeping silently behind her. By the time they'd visited the bridge, been given a glimpse of the Captain's quarters, and returned to the deck, Bundo had moved away.

"I would dearly love to see the engine." The prince looked ready to bounce on his toes with eagerness.

"This way." Cal led them into the depths of the ship. Joliu started and looked uncertainly at the Prince.

"I am aware the Sombi were the ones to settle Finches Harbour. That was so many generations back, no sensible person can hold you responsible for their enmity. I visited your home. It is both a beautiful and peaceful place."

Joliu breathed out in relief and proceeded to give a detailed explanation of the steam tank and the engine. The prince grinned throughout, then to Joliu's shock shook his hand and thanked him.

At the top of the gangway, Roger once again kissed her hand, then walked away with Chiza following.

"Visiting royalty?" Paul leaned on the rail and watched them as the crowd parted in front of them.

"The third prince. His name's Roger."

"I thought I was joking." Paul glanced over at her. "I want to thank you for not busting my chops at the White Moby. I about died when you walked in."

"You were on shore leave; I wasn't about to interfere with your fun." Cal turned around at looked up at the stack. "I enjoyed your story." Her stomach twinged, the prince had hinted at someone who would be glad to kill Bundo. "Pull up the gangway. We'll let the rest board with the ladder. I want the watch doubled until we sail." Cal left Paul with his mouth open and climbed back down to the engine room to tell Joliu to build the steam to full readiness.

She went to her cabin to change into her uniform and found the tiny silk rug lying on her bed. Cal laughed in delight and ran her hands across the beautifully dyed, finely-woven surface before rolling it up and stowing it safely.

# Chapter 2 - The Zithayan Dynasty

The Kestrel sailed with the sun peeking over the horizon. Jorges reported the night passed quietly but for a few drunken stevedores who staggered past in the dark.

The next stop was an easy three-day steam. Having reloaded at Lusundi, they didn't need any stores at Klixxe.

"This is a very different place," Lord Sifton had said. "Slavers and worse prowl the streets. Keep your people close."

On the Lord's advice, Cal didn't allow any shore leave. Whatever she thought of the man, he knew the country better than she did.

Since Bundo agreed with the man's assessment; the crew spent two days making minor repairs to the Kestrel. Cal sat on the bridge with her sketchbook trying to capture the scene of the prince laughing in delight. She didn't think her drawing did him justice.

They travelled up the coast of Harasah to where it turned east and became the continent of Zithay. The ports and their residents changed. Roofs were tile instead of thatch. Rice and noodles replaced bread as a staple.

One evening they steamed past a wall which had to be at least the height of Lord Carroway's mansion. It continued on the other side of the mouth of the harbour, thicker than the Kestrel was long. Cal suspected it circled most of the city.

"There are chains which can be raised to block the mouth of the harbour." Lord Sifton walked up to stand beside Cal on the bridge. She'd given up telling him he needed to be invited. "The place is safe enough if you obey the laws. Near the docks, they make allowances for foreigners. On the hill, you insult the wrong person, and you are dead on the street." He pointed to a steamship tied up to one side of the huge harbour. "The Zithayan Dynasty won't allow anyone to build an embassy *in* the city, so the Anglian embassy is on that ship. There are others outside the walls. If there is real trouble don't try to flee, get over to the embassy ship and stay there."

Cal glared at his back. She didn't like him, something about him bothered her. For a science expedition, they spent a lot of time in port. Stops to gather samples were perfunctory at best. Whatever he was up to, Cal didn't believe it was science. What few samples they'd put in the crates in stowage would answer her questions, but her contract forbade her doing more than seeing the sample safely stored.

"Jorges, the bridge door stays locked from now on. I'm tired of him making himself at home. Pass the word to the others."

"Aye." Jorges grinned at her.

Cal climbed down to the deck and gazed at Puhkan. According to the maps, it was not the largest port in the Dynasty. However, for the western countries like Anglia, it was the most important.

"Gather the crew," Cal called to Paul.

When they crowded around her in the mess, Cal counted her people and the ones who were missing. Thomas at the bottom of the ocean, Henrichs and the purser in Malacca with the fever. Her crew waited patiently, not one nervous face among them. Damn this is a good crew, Cal thought.

"The scientists are off doing what they do. I believe it's time to clear a few things up. First, I have the best crew aboard anything that floats. Don't you forget it! You know we're running short. Franz is apprenticing in the engine room. Joliu tells me you're about ready for your pin. Good work. Paul has been picking up the slack as acting Mate since I got bumped to Captain. I appreciate you haven't given him any trouble. I think it's time to make it official, so Paul, you are now the Second Mate of the Kestrel." Cal waited for the cheers and back slapping to die down. "I would say you all owe him a drink, but since he's never been known to pay for a drink..." Paul laughed and gave a thumbs-up.

"I considered bringing people on to fill Thomas' place on the roster and give Bundo more time for his work as purser. Perhaps on the voyage home." Cal took the time to meet each person's eyes. "There is something off with this voyage. I hope I'm wrong but stay alert. Don't wander off alone and no trouble. If you must get drunk, do it on board. If you see something that bothers you, report it to me or Paul. Don't care how trivial it is." She listened to the muttering. Concerns, but no complaints.

"Last thing. The gangway stays up unless it is being used. Double the watch while we're on shore, but I don't want the second person to be obvious. I'll leave it up to you how."

Cal saluted the crew.

"Dismissed."

They wandered off, some talking to Bundo about the shore rotation.

"I didn't expect a promotion." Paul came over to her. "My entire repertoire of officer jokes is now useless."

Cal laughed and slapped him on the back. "I'm sure you'll find new ones."

A few of the crew went down the rope ladder to the dock. Cal pulled out her sketchbook and tried to lose herself in drawing. After a few desultory attempts, she put the paper and pencils away and laid down in her cabin.

Quiet knocking woke her.

"Yes?" Cal rolled to her feet. "What is it?"

"No emergency," Paul's voice came through the door. "But you may want to join me for tea in the mess."

"Give me five." Cal scurried to get dressed. At least the Captain's uniform went on quickly. Only in the most desperate of situations would she go out on deck in her nightgown.

"Okay," Cal slid in across from Paul and Jorges. She picked up the tea Paul pushed toward her. "What is important enough to wake me?"

"The Kestrel is being watched." Jorges shook his head. "Checked around the other ships, nothing out of line, just ours."

"How many?"

"Four I counted, but from their placement, there's likely more. I spotted them on the way out. When I didn't see any surveillance on other ships, I watched closer on my way back to the ship. 'Fraid I acted the drunk, so you'll obviously need to give me punishment duty."

Cal studied Jorges' face. He wasn't scared, just doing what his captain asked him.

"Sounds like you did some training."

"A couple of years in Naval intelligence. When I had to muster out, Henrichs offered me the berth on the Kestrel."

"Very good. Jorges, keep it low key and don't put yourself or anyone else at risk, but I'd like you to gather what intelligence you can. Report to Paul, he'll decide whether to bring me in."

Jorges nodded briskly, Paul a little reluctantly.

"Paul, if Jorges keeps running to the Captain, someone will spot it and make trouble. Trust your instincts. Err on the side of caution."

Cal left the men in the mess and carried her mug out on deck. She leaned against the rail and sipped at the tea while admiring the lights of the city. When the cup was empty, Cal went back to bed.

***

Nothing happened for the next week. Jorges confirmed the watchers were still there, so it was more than just curiosity. Meanwhile, Paul told his stories in bars and collected stories from others. Jorge mopped the deck and complained about losing his rotation ashore.

Neither Lord Sifton or any of the scientists had shown up. Cal drummed her fingers on the helm. The contract was clear. Lord Sifton commanded his team, which meant no interference from the Captain while they were on land, but she didn't want to be stuck here much longer. Time to get some advice.

Cal put on her dress whites and blue jacket, then strolled down the dock to pay a visit to the embassy ship. Bundo accompanied her, craning his neck at the sights as they walked.

"Captain Shillingsworth of HMSV Kestrel," she introduced herself to the pair of guards at the foot of the stairs they'd let down from the ship. It could have fit Kestrel in its hold with room to spare. "I would like to pay a courtesy call on the ambassador as it looks like we'll be in port a while yet."

"Follow me." One of the men led the way, the steps vibrating under his best parade march. Cal and Bundo followed more quietly. A woman met them at the top of the stairs, nodding at the guard who then returned to his post.

Does she wait for the sound of stomping feet? Cal tried to imagine how they could code the noise for different situations.

"...is busy, but the Captain would be pleased to meet with you in the officer's mess."

"Very well." *Don't lose focus,* Cal admonished herself. The woman led them through passageways which, if Cal hadn't known they were aboard a ship, could have been any government office. Bundo was dropped off at the enlisted mess, with instructions to a nearby sailor keep him company. They climbed stairs to an oaken door. Cal's guide knocked, then pushed the door open and waved Cal in.

"Welcome, Captain." The Captain of the embassy ship wore enough gold braid to sink the Kestrel. His mouth smiled, however, his eyes reserved judgement. Since the man reached out a hand, Cal shook it. "Won't stand on ceremony here. I'm Captain Jenkins Hashmick, his Majesty's Navy."

"Captain Calliope Shillingsworth, of his Majesty's Science Vessel Kestrel."

Jenkins handed her a snifter with amber brandy in it. "Heard you were a brandy drinker."

Cal swirled the glass and took in the rich odour, then tasted it.

"I'd go bankrupt if I developed a taste for this." She sipped at it again and let out a long sigh.

"Captain Cully is an old friend, and I have other sources who tell me you are an extraordinary young woman. Made a Lady of the Realm and the first Royal Engineer appointed by the Crown Prince. Rarified territory even for an old hand like me."

"I won't say it was luck, but I had the best teachers."

"I've been hearing stories about you going through the Gates of Hell?"

"Our contract included it in the voyage. They paid a considerable bonus for the privilege."

"I'm not surprised you made it through, you have a good head on your shoulders. What shocked me was hearing that you stopped and picked up a man overboard midway through the worst stretch."

"The man was the one paying the bills."

Jenkins roared with laughter and waved at her glass. "Drink up and I'll refill it."

"It would be sacrilege to guzzle this elixir."

"Tell me about the Gates." He topped up his glass and swirled it.

"Going east, the first bit wasn't as bad as storms we've weathered in the north." Cal smiled at Jenkins' doubtful look. "Once we passed Sea Devil's Island, things got interesting. I had everyone, crew and passengers both, tied down. I was strapped to the helm. Even with me picking the softest path, I've never experienced any stretch of water so violent. Without being tied down, I'd have lost my crew to broken bones."

"Standard procedure if a Navy vessel needs to go through the Gates. Can't remember the last one to make the trip." Captain Jenkins took a long sip at his brandy. "It is also standing orders that no ship is to attempt a rescue in the Gates. Good thing you aren't naval or you'd be up before a review board."

"To be honest, Sir, it wasn't a conscious decision." Cal told him the story then stared into her brandy as she swirled it. "If I had it to do again, I would have cut off my reaction and left him behind, and not just because he's a twit. This is my first voyage as Captain. I'm supposed to be First Mate and learning the ropes. Captain Henrichs took a fever and left me in charge. I would fully support a review board removing my command." To Cal's horror, a tear dropped into her brandy. "It's immaterial that I succeeded, the risk was too great on top of the already dangerous conditions."

"Drink up, Captain. That's an order."

Cal sipped down the brandy and let its fire burn to her gut. Captain Jenkins poured her another glass.

"You just proved you're the right person to captain your ship. I ran aground on my first command. It isn't the stupid things we inevitably do, it's whether we learn from them. Yours might have been harder than most, but if I were on the review board, I'd be recommending you go back to First Mate as planned, then take another run at Captain when you're ready."

"Thank you, Sir." Cal took another gulp of brandy. "That's what I'm going to ask when we get back to port."

"I could send a man to command you home." Captain Jenkins tilted his head and lifted his eyebrows.

This is a test, forget about what he wants me to say. What do I need to do? Cal sighed and put her glass on the table beside her chair.

"The crew trusts me; a new command would be disruptive. However, if you happen to have someone who needs passage home, any advice they give would be most welcome."

"My dear, if you get tired of civilian command, we can use good officers in the Navy."

Cal looked at him unable to keep the shock off her face. If she hadn't put her glass down she might have slugged it back to give herself time to think.

"Let me put it this way, Captain; the Navy needs people who can think on their feet and make tough calls. People only get that way with training and experience. The fact you're willing to take on someone to offer advice shows determination to learn. That you don't hand over your command tells me you have gumption and the will to see things through. It so happens I do have a man who needs to get back to Anglia. He's smart enough to know when to offer advice and when to keep his mouth shut. One of our best trainers before the Ambassador snatched him up for this detail."

"I would like to meet him."

"I'll send him over to visit." Jenkins picked up her glass and handed it back to her. "Now, about the reason you came here." He made drinking motions with his hand.

"I refuse to stagger back to my ship." Cal sniffed at the brandy and regretfully put it back on the table. "The passengers who hired my ship did so saying they were scientists. They planned to survey species along the east shore of Harasah and beyond. I don't think they are doing that. I have my suspicions as to what they are about. If I'm right, my interference could get them killed or captured. If I'm wrong, they've been gone more than a week without so much as a runner, and it may be time to set a search in motion."

"Your Lord Sifton is a shady one. I haven't heard anything official, but there are stories. Now you're the Captain. What are your responsibilities to this man?"

"According to the contract, I command the ship, he commands the team and determines the course and timing of the voyage. My concern is for my ship and crew. My gut tells me this is more dangerous than the Gates of Hell. The Kestrel is being watched. My crew is sure they are being followed on shore leave. Something has the Zithayan Dynasty worried.  My instinct is to weigh anchor and head home. It isn't good for the crew to stagnate this long, especially if the situation is delicate. What I keep coming up against is I don't like the man, and maybe it's colouring my judgement."

"People like Sifton make a career out of landing on their feet. The folks around them usually aren't so lucky. From what you said about the contract, you're stuck waiting unless something urgent comes up. But if the situation deteriorates, I'll figure something out. In the meantime, waiting is the hardest part of life."

"True." Cal stood up and checked that the floor didn't tilt under her. "Thank you for the talk and the brandy."

"When you get home, look up the Naval Academy, tell them I sent you. Better yet, I'll give you a letter of introduction. We may be able to steal you yet." Captain Jenkins stood and saluted and Cal returned it. He accompanied her down to where she picked Bundo up. They walked back to the Kestrel, Cal deep in thought.

# Chapter 3 - Trouble

Jorges waited for her in the mess. He held a cup of tea, but his tight posture betrayed his tension.

Cal fetched herself a cup, then sat down across from him.

"You learn anything from your punishment duty?" She gave him a stern look.

"Yes Ma'am." Jorges hung his head and twisted the still full cup in his hand. "I found a tea room. Can't get drunk on tea, Ma'am, and the people don't laugh at me, much."

"Never mind, it's better than them beating on you." Cal picked up the cup as Jorges whispered.

"Leave in fifteen minutes. Dress like a sailor. I'll find you."

Cal rinsed the mugs out and left them to dry. In her cabin, she opened a drawer she didn't use much these days. The outfit Pentam had given her, a couple of years back now would do nicely. It still was stained and greasy. She put it on quickly and topped it off with her cap. A swipe of her fingers and her face became black smudged.

Out on deck, Paul stood with a list checking out the crew headed for shore.

"You're late, Sailor." He frowned at her. "I've half a mind to hold you back." Then he waved his hand as if she'd said something. "Oh get on, but don't come back drunk."

Cal hid a smile as she walked down the gangway. Paul hoisted it up behind her. Jorges hadn't said what direction to walk, so she headed toward the tavern the crew went to.

"Heh, I'm tired of the same old thing." Jorges came out of an alley adjusting his pants. "I found this place, the girls are friendly."

Cal shrugged and Jorges led her up past the tavern, through an alley to another street, this one with fewer foreigners on it. She looked closely at the people. Just like at a market on the continent, there were all kinds of outfits from pragmatic to extravagant. The people themselves looked different enough to have come from different countries. She didn't know much about the Dynasty, but she'd heard it was the union of many tribes. Some were as dark as Bundo, while a few had almost white hair and blue eyes. The right clothing, the right knowledge, and an Anglian would be able to move about freely.

Jorges nodded to their right and they walked into a tea room. Cal had expected something dainty and bright, but this place looked as rough as the tavern. Men and women sat or knelt at low tables, some talking animatedly, others alone staring into their cups as if the world's wisdom would be found there.

In one corner, his hair long and straggly, a rough beard holding the remains of supper, sat a man Cal recognized. His blue eyes widened and he started to stand. Cal sat on one side, Jorges on the other.

"I believe I've met your cousin, Bri." Cal spoke quietly, but not in a whisper. Bri slumped back, then shrugged and grinned.

"Bit of a stuffed shirt that one, always looking to avoid risk. Should have been an accountant."

One of the girls came over and bowed. Jorges said something in a halting manner which made the girl's face turn a little pink, but she bowed again and left.

Bri examined Jorges, then Cal.

"I'm guessing you're not here for the tea."

"You can't imagine how tired I am of the tea in the ship's galley." Cal looked over at where the girl loaded a tray with a teapot and tiny handleless cups.

She came back to serve them, giggling a bit at Jorges.

"I'll have to remember that one," Bri picked up a cup and tasted. He sighed. "I could never order this and get away with it." Cal and Jorges followed suit. The tea, which was coloured a pale, golden green, was of superb quality. A fresh, delicate aroma rose gently from the teacup into her nose as Cal took a sip.

"Let's cut out the chit-chat," Bri's voice grew sharp even as his face stayed amiable.

"I'm not interested in what you are doing." Cal swirled the tea like brandy. "Don't expect you'd share your countries secrets any more than I'd share mine."

Bri nodded and relaxed a bit more.

"What I would like is your professional opinion of Lord Sifton."

"He's a cad and would slit your throat if he thought it would profit him. Guess he had to use his own name to hire you so he could play scientist. Watch your back around him. He is probably after the same thing as I am, and half-dozen other agents. Rumour has it one of the Dynasty scientists has tamed lightning and can make it on demand. Not sure what use it would be, some kind of machine is the scuttlebutt. All the attention has got Dynasty security nervous. More than one person has shown up dead in a trash heap. At least one of Sifton's men took a dagger to the heart. Told me before he died, they'd seen the thing and even got a sketch. Had nothing on him, or I'd be long gone. My guess is Sifton is holed up waiting for the heat to die down or focus on someone else."

"Sounds like him; he knows his goods, but has no heart to temper him." Cal drank more tea, then refilled her cup. "If it isn't giving up state secrets, what is it like living in your home?"

"It's home." Bri absently filled his cup and slopped tea on the table. "Mountains stretch to the sky, valleys as green as emeralds. The cities are old as the hills but filled with gardens and the sound of children laughing."

"Sounds lovely. I'll have to visit sometime."

"Sadly, I don't think it would be wise." Bri met her eyes. "The new emperor is not content with what he has. I don't like it, but no one asks people like me their opinion."

"I see." Cal half grinned. "Until we are officially enemies, I will count you as a friend." The light dimmed as men came into the room.

"Time to go," Jorges said quietly. "The men who came in are trouble. They work as muscle for the gangs, and hire out to take contract work."

"Drink your tea. Laugh a little." Bri put his hand on Cal's arm. "Wait until they sit before you leave. Don't look at them as you leave."

Cal followed his instructions. She got up and slapped Jorges on the shoulder. He groaned and pushed to his feet. On the way out, he waved at the serving girl and she blushed again.

"They're following us, probably plan to jump us in the alley. There may be people waiting there to cut us off."

"Suggestions?"

"If it was just me, I'd let them attack and see what I learned from them."

"Let's do that. Real sailors wouldn't suddenly change their route anyway."

They walked and shoved at each other laughing as Jorges told horribly dirty jokes. As they ducked into the alley, Cal snuck a peek behind her. Three men sauntered in their direction. Even the most confident thugs would want better odds.

Cal tapped three times on Jorges' arm. He tapped twice back. The slap of a shoe on the cobbles alerted her. She turned to face the three while Jorges faced the other way. A couple of thumps and grunts were the only indication battle had been joined. Cal kicked some refuse at the three coming at her. She had no idea how to fight; it had never seemed important.

The lead man grinned wolfishly at her. He stretched out his steps to carry him ahead of his companions. Jorges spun Cal around and met the eager thug with a kick to his throat. The man went down with a gurgle. Two men lay bonelessly on the pavement. She turned again in time to see a shadow drop behind the last two before they fell forward to lie still.

The whole thing had taken seconds.

"Good work," Jorges grinned at Bundo before kneeling to search through the attackers' clothing. "Pros won't carry anything to identify them or their employer, but it never hurts to check." He rolled one over and paper rustled under the dead man's shirt. Jorges pulled it out and handed it to Cal. She tucked it in a pocket. "Let's go."

At the other end of the alley, a man lay slumped against the wall. Blood turned his shirt black.  The attackers had probably taken the paper from him before taking the opportunity to eliminate Cal and Jorges. Cal stepped over him to follow Jorges. Bundo had vanished again. A group of sailors left the tavern.

"From the ship two down from us," Jorges muttered, meaning the sailors. He pulled Cal up to tag along at the back of the group. None of the men noticed. Cal missed their presences as she and Jorges walked toward the Kestrel.

They weren't more than twenty yards from the ship when several men stepped out of the shadows on a path to intercept them.

"Sailors!" Paul shouted from the deck. "You're late. The Captain is going to have your ass." Joliu and Hank joined him at the rail to shout at them.

"People like you are what get us all locked on the ship." Jorges pulled Cal along as if the men weren't there. When Cal chanced a glance around, they were gone.

Paul tossed the rope ladder over for them. Once on the ship, he rounded on them.

"I warned you what would happen if you were late again. Didn't I?"

"Yes, Sir!" The men shouted.

"I'm going to be kind to you and not wake the Captain, but you'll be polishing brass all day tomorrow."

Cal grinned at him and winked before Joliu hauled her away talking about work needing doing in the engine room and when was she planning to do that if she were polishing the Captain's brass.

Once inside and down the ladder to the engine room, Cal allowed herself to relax.

"Turn up the lantern." She pulled the paper from her pocket and peered at it. It looked like someone had asked a chicken to copy a drawing. She could make out there were two 'C' shaped things around a central core. It looked like the core was supposed to spin on its long axis. Lines led from the 'C' shaped things. Now that she looked closer it looked like they were wrapped in something. Markings which might have been labels in Dynasty script were scattered about the page.

Shouting sounded from on deck.

Cal put the paper into the fire and shut the door.

"If that's what I think it is, we don't want that paper anywhere on board. You go first and let me slip to my cabin."

Joliu nodded and scampered up the ladder. He paused a moment in the hatch to the deck as

Cal ran to her cabin. She'd barely closed the door behind her when a fist thumped on it.

"Captain, some folks are demanding to see you, now."

"Be right out." Cal changed into her Captain's uniform and used her rag with turpentine on it to clean her face. A last look in the mirror to set her cranky Captain's face and Cal stormed out onto the deck.

"What in blazes is so important it can't wait until morning." Paul pointed over the rail and Cal stomped over to look. A man in a uniform glared up at them, flanked by men dressed in the same loose black clothing as the ones in the alley. "Who are you and why are you disturbing my ship?"

"Five men were found dead in an alley not far from here. I was told two of your crew were late. I want to question them." The man struck a pose which suggested he was used to immediate obedience.

"Why?"

"If they attacked and killed citizens of—"

Cal roared with laughter.

"You think Oswald and Jorges could take on five men? Only reason Os is still on the ship is he's small and useful in the engine room. He couldn't kill five flies never mind men. Jorges is a sailor, not a soldier."

"Yet, even so, I demand—"

"You demand? You demand? Did you see the fight? Any witnesses? No? Then go away and let me sleep. Keep a watch on the wharf if you must, but you aren't stepping foot on one of His Majesty's ships on some flimsy excuse. Probably one of you is an engineer and you want to steal the design of a good Anglian engine."

The man stared at Cal with his mouth open, then turned to snarl instructions at the men before stomping off.

Cal turned from the rail and lambasted Paul and Hank until she figured the official was out of hearing. She finished with orders to toss Os in the brig for causing trouble and marched back to her cabin. Bundo waited for her, dripping on the floor.

"Good." Cal sat in her chair and let out her breath. "What a fiasco. I'm sure they'll be back with reinforcements. If they want on the ship, there's nothing we can do to stop them."

"The paper is important?"

"A diagram for a machine. I studied it and burned it. Go through the ship. Anything which might cause trouble gets disposed of. I'm taking no chances. First thing in the morning, signal the embassy ship." She smiled up at him. "Thank you, Bundo. I knew I could rely on you to keep me safe."

Bundo grinned and bowed.

"One last thing." Cal handed him the clothing and cap she'd worn on shore. "Put this and some other things in one of the empty crew berths. Make it look used. We'll need someone to play Os in the brig. Maybe Franz can do it; they haven't seen him yet." Bundo nodded and left, closing the door gently behind him. Cal closed and fastened the porthole. The only one on the ship to open. Too filled with adrenaline to sleep, Cal lay on the bed and plotted.

***

At mid-morning, the official from the previous night returned in the company of an older man in an elaborate uniform.

"Many apologies," the official called up. "We are searching all the ships." He pointed down the dock where other groups of officials were being allowed on board. "It is a customs inspection." He stared at her with a completely blank expression.

"Customs?" Cal rolled her eyes. "Drop the gangway for these gentlemen, Second Mate. Then go make fresh tea." She was certain the official paled a little; he must have had Anglian tea before.

When the men reached the deck, Cal stepped forward and bowed low to the official. "My apologies. I am not at my best when freshly woken. I hope I didn't offend."

He bowed in return but didn't speak.

"Let us begin." The older official took out a notebook and pencil. "You may not be aware, but we've had problems with art being stolen and smuggled out of the country. All art for export will be stamped with a red seal."

"Very well."

Cal spent the rest of the day watching the two men very thoroughly inspect every nook and cranny of the ship. They opened each crate in the hold and picked through their contents. Cal ground her teeth as she took note of what looked nothing like scientific samples. There were rocks and bits of wood, dried herbs and odd contraptions, little of it labelled as it should be. Franz sealed up each crate as the officials were finished with them.

She convinced them to take tea and scones with her and Paul. They didn't touch the tea but finished off the scones and jam. When she was escorting them off the ship, Cookie ran out to hand them a wrapped bundle of still warm scones.

"Cap'n said you liked them."

The older official smiled and bowed as he took the bundle, then led the way down to the dock.

The next morning, a young boy hailed them from the dock and pantomimed giving the package in his hand to the ship. Cal had the gangway lowered and waved the boy up. He looked around with wide eyes before bowing and handing her the package. As soon as Cal took it, the boy fled. She sniffed and sighed.

"Tea."

The boy had hardly disappeared when Captain Jenkins hailed them from the dock. He was accompanied by a grizzled man in an immaculate dress uniform.

"Permission to come aboard."

"Permission granted, and welcome." Cal handed the package to Jorges. "Go make some for us."

"Quite the show last night." Captain Jenkins looked around the ship. "Guards told me they heard every word." He grinned at her. "Good job. Letting them on board and plying them with help and food was even better. Keep them confused." He waved the other man forward. He stood no taller than Cal but exuded competence and danger.

"Commander McAllen," the man introduced himself. Cal put out her hand and he took it with a firm grip. "Captain Jenkins informs me you have a berth for me to return to Anglia. Received notice my son was in an accident. Family over duty."

"It will be our pleasure to have you aboard. Paul here's my Second Mate; he'll show you to a berth. I can send a couple of men to bring anything you need from the Embassy."

"No need, it is being packed and brought over as we speak."

"Captain, I know you are waiting for your passengers, but I will take responsibility for them. Please make the best time you can back to Anglia." Captain Jenkins saluted and Cal returned it.

Two burly sailors hoisted a trunk up the gangway. Cal pointed them toward where Paul had headed with the Commander. One handed Captain Jenkins a bottle.

"A small thank you." Captain Jenkins passed it to her. "Maybe you'll be kind enough to share it with the commander."

Cal wanted to hug the bottle but made do with grinning and nodding.

Captain Jenkins collected his sailors and headed down the gangway.

"Make her ready to sail. I want to watch the sunset from the open sea." Cal called to her crew who immediately burst into organized activity. She leaned against the rail and watched.

"Pardon, Captain." A young man stood on the dock. "Message." He held out a piece of paper. Cal walked down and took it, read it, then tossed it into the water.

Sifton. The man wanted a meeting with her immediately.

"Bundo." Cal waved to him. "Let's go for a walk."

They didn't have far to go to find the seedy tavern mentioned in Sifton's message. She led the way in and took a seat in a corner. Bundo waved down a server and snagged a couple of tankards.

They hadn't been there long before a grimy beggar sidled up to them

"What the hell do you think you're doing?" Sifton hissed.

"Meeting exactly as you requested."

"Anyone with common sense—"

"If you wanted something different, you should have been clear. Talk quickly."

"You must stay another week. One of my men got hold of a piece of information which could change everything."

"I've been ordered back to Anglia at all speed." Cal pushed the tankard away and wiped her fingers on her pants.

"You don't take orders from Jenkins, you take my orders." Sifton talked loud enough for heads to turn in their direction.

"Wrong." Cal caught his eyes and held them. "I reread the contract. You misrepresented yourself and your purpose. In that circumstance, the Captain is free to take whatever action she feels appropriate. You've endangered my ship and my crew. I'm sure the Embassy will help you."

"I can ruin you, Captain. You do what I—"

"Sorry, I don't care what kind of sob story you feed me." Cal stood up as she spoke loud enough to be heard through the room. "I don't give money to beggars or thieves." She wiped her hands on her pants again, then left. Bundo followed.

"He's trouble."

"But he's not my trouble, not any longer."

"He'll find a way. His kind always does."

As soon as the gangway was hoisted up behind Cal, they cast off the ropes and steamed away.

# Chapter 4 - Trouble comes to roost

After months at sea, the Kestrel returned to port in Anglia. They'd picked up Henrichs on the way home. The purser had fallen for a tavern keeper's widow and stayed behind. Henrichs refused to resume command, grinning wickedly as she talked with the Commander on deck. Cal pushed away her irritation and did what she had to.

"I will be taking extended shore leave while the Kestrel is being refitted. Joliu wants to tinker with the coal feeder. Thinks we need a better crusher to handle all the different qualities of coal. If it isn't too much for you, keep an eye on him. I don't want to need a bigger ship to hold the engine."

"Aye, Ma'am." Henrichs snapped to attention, her eyes glinting with humour.

Cal glared at her. "I will return as First Mate, or not at all."

"Cal, you can't go backwards. Trust me. Hire a First Mate with lots of experience you can trust. There's no reason they have to be younger than you." Henrichs coughed and went pale. "I'm not sure I'll be going back to sea. That fever stole something from me and I'm not young anymore."

"Then you'd better be on the lookout for suitable Mates."

"Aye, Ma'am." Henrichs enveloped Cal in a hug. "You did a damn good job, Cal. Don't let anyone tell you different."

Cal hoisted her belongings, leaving Henrichs with the Kestrel. She looked back, the old girl tugging at her heart. Maybe Henrichs was right.

She caught a train into the city. Outside the window, the trees passing by were just budding into green.

The taxi dropped her off at the gate of the home she shared with her father.

"Hello, Hans." Cal stuck her head into the stable. "How's the new engine running?"

"How did you know we had a new engine?" Hans pushed his hair back with a greasy hand. "It's supposed to be more efficient, but I don't know."

"I'll come to have a look at it after I've said hello to Father."

Hans looked like he wanted to say something, but nodded instead.

Cal walked into the house and carried her gear up to her room where she washed up quickly and changed into what she thought of as her civilian clothes. She found her father in his office surrounded by ledgers and drawings.

"How's the memoir coming?" Cal asked and gave her father a kiss on the cheek. He looked up at her, worry clouding his face for a moment before he smiled.

"I continue to be amazed I survived to be an old man." Sir Shillingsworth pushed a journal aside. "I took some terrifying risks in my youth." He waved for Cal to sit. "I can't tell you how helpful it is to have your drawings to remind me of things. Memory changes in a way paper and pencil do not." He pushed a paper over to her. "This is your earliest drawing of my work that I could find."

"I remember this," Cal looked at the careful picture of a skull with predator's teeth in a perpetual snarl. "I snuck into the room and drew this. I was bored with flowers and fruit. You were furious, but the next day you asked me to do more, and I never stopped."

"So tell me, what kind of art were you able to do as a First Mate?"

"Actually, I was Captain for most of the voyage. Henrichs stayed ashore with a fever."

"Yes, I remember now, you mentioned something about it in a letter," her father put a hand to his head as if he was in pain.

"Are you all right, Father?" Cal's heart ached.

"Just tired, Cal." He smiled at her. "Let the old man see what you did while you were away."

Cal brought out a sketchbook and they spent the time until Beth called them for supper talking about her drawings and the voyage.

***

"Lord Carroway sends his compliments and asks you to come to a gathering at his estate. He's delighted you've returned." Sir Shillingsworth passed Cal the letter over breakfast.

"Will Pentam be there?"

"He and Crysabel are away at her father's estate. She's expecting and her mother wants her close by. Pentam is using the time to work on his thesis."

"He's finally going to do it, is he?" Cal put the letter down, enjoying the feel of the quality paper between her fingers. If only she could afford to draw on such fine material.

"Yes, he'll be Dr. Booksdale before the year is out. Even Gostan has given up and admitted the boy is brilliant."

"That's wonderful. Maybe I'll have time to make a trip out to see them." Cal stood and picked up Lord Carroway's letter. "I'll let Lord Carroway know I'll be attending his gathering."

"Gathering? Oh, yes, of course." Sir Shillingsworth got up. "I'll be working in my study."

Cal watched him limp away, a crease of worry on her brow. She scribbled a response to Lord Carroway, then took it out to Hans.

"Please deliver it this morning."

Hans nodded and started the fire on the one steam carriage that wasn't in pieces all over the stable.

She poked through the remaining parts, imagining how they'd go together. They were a trade-off. Less coal to heat the water, but a shorter range since the water tank was smaller. She saw some interesting ways the maker had used to seal the pistons better so not as much steam was used. It did make the engine more complicated and likely to break down so it wouldn't work on the Kestrel. She needed an engine which worked under all conditions; losing some efficiency was a small price to pay to know they'd always have power.

Cal went back inside and organized her sketchbooks from the trip. She had books covering the better part of a wall in the room she used as a studio when she was home. Except for the ones her father had out, these represented all the years of Cal's art. She left one book out and took it over to her desk. The entire book was filled with her attempts to recreate the drawing she'd burned on the Kestrel. The task was made more difficult because she had no idea what it represented or what the scale of it was. She looked through the book, then closed it and sighed. Maybe Pentam could make something of it. Chemistry was his expertise; he might be able to figure something out.

Another book lay open on her desk. It overflowed with drawings of airships. Renditions of what she remembered of her first sighting a couple of years ago, to her imaginings of what she might build. Her notes covered the gamut from materials to the equations telling her the ratio between the size of the airship and how much it could lift. It would have to float in the air like the Kestrel floated on the ocean. She'd seen paper lanterns which, lit by a candle, floated away into the sky. Cal went to get the book where she'd drawn one in detail and added it to her idea journal. How on earth could she heat the volume of air needed to lift an airship?

Beth, their cook and housekeeper, knocked on the door and called her down for lunch. With her father still working in his office, she was alone.

"Sit down and join me." Cal waved a chair. "It's just us." She served up a bowl and placed it in front the woman who was family in Cal's mind if not in hers.

"He's been working harder on his book." Beth tasted her soup and nodded absently. "Except when Hans or I drag him out of there, he hardly moves. I think he'd sleep there if we let him."

"Maybe he'll let me read more of his book." Cal took a bit of buttered bread and closed her eyes. Such simple things she missed on board her ship.

"Oh no, he won't let anyone see it." Beth frowned. "He was furious one day when he thought I was trying to peek at it. I haven't touched anything in his study since."

"That doesn't sound like Father." Cal looked over at Beth. "He said he's fine, but something doesn't feel right. Keep an eye on him, will you? Make sure he eats and sleeps properly."

"I will, Miss."

***

The carriage dropped Cal off in front of Lord Carroway's. The steam carriage had been acting up, so she'd hired an old-fashioned horse-drawn vehicle.

Lord Carroway's butler took her wrap.

"Welcome back to Anglia, Lady Shillingsworth."

"Thank you, it is good to see different faces for a while."

A maid guided her to the ballroom and left her at the door. Cal walked through into the crowded room where an orchestra played music in the background. Ladies in fine gowns walked about the room with fingertips on the arms of their men, looking like peacocks beside crows.

Cal wandered over to chat with a woman who was a casual friend of Crysabel's; maybe she'd know how her friend was doing. The woman saw Cal coming and turned her back. All around other men and women were turning away from Cal, leaving her in a bubble of isolation in the room.

"My dear Cal." Lord Carroway appeared beside her and took her elbow. "Come with me a moment." He frowned at the people around him. "I never thought." Cal looked down at him and thought he was on the edge of tears. "I'm sorry, there is a horrible person talking about you."

"Lord Sifton." Cal's stomach clenched.

"He's hinting at things..." Lord Carroway put his hand on his chest. "I don't believe a word he says, but some are easily influenced. Scandal is the hobby of the nobility."

"I see." Cal forced the acid burning in her gut down. "I survived most of my life being a failure as a Lady, I expect I can survive this too."

"Lady Shillingsworth." Lord Sifton's voice dripped venom.

Cal turned and pasted a smile on her face.

"How good to see you. I'm glad the Embassy was able to help you."

"You mean after you turned tail and ran, leaving me behind without a second thought? I had to take a train across the continent to get home."

"If that is how you wish to describe it." Cal shrugged. "I long ago ceased to care what you thought of me."

"I've lodged a complaint with the merchant's board, breach of contract, cowardice." Lord Sifton smiled. "They were quite concerned."

"I can imagine." Cal walked over to help herself to a glass of wine. She needed something in her hand to keep her from smacking the man. "My employers are also *very* concerned. They are examining the log book and the cargo. The Zithayan's did a customs inspection on every ship in port. They opened all the crates in the hold. It was that or have them seized. Imagine my employers' distress at learning, not one held anything remotely connected to the expedition you told them you were planning."

Lord Sifton's face turned red.

"Those crates are mine. You have no right to open them."

"I don't, but customs and my employers do. Especially since I filed a complaint for breach of contract with them before coming to the city. I guess we will have to wait for the court to pick through everything and come to a decision. In the meantime, I'm so glad to see you looking healthy. How are the men who accompanied you on the expedition?"

Cal hoped Sifton would drop dead from the purple of his face.

"None of them were able to escape, thanks to your desertion."

"It is too bad, but as you pointed out when I had to bury a crewmember at sea—it is what they were paid for, is it not?"

Cal nodded at him and wandered away. The people in the room openly pointed at her, muttering and frowning. A woman bumped into Cal, spilling wine on Cal's gown, hissing at her some indecipherable complaint. Cal took the excuse to make her exit.

***

There were no more invitations to events after that. Cal worked in her studio, scratching out ideas for airships. After three days, she screamed and threw her pencil across the room.

"I am going to visit Crysabel," she told her father at supper.

"Okay, I will see you tomorrow." Lord Shillingsworth ate a piece of the fish from his plate.

"She's at her father's estate in the country. I'll be gone at least a week."

"Oh yes, of course." He reddened in embarrassment and looked away.

Cal almost cancelled her plans out of worry for her father. Something was certainly wrong... however, Beth convinced her to go.

Cal boarded the train with a small bag, wearing a plain travelling gown. She wasn't in the mood to be recognized and snubbed. Her response to Lord Sifton had been a three-quarters bluff. The people who'd backed Lord Sifton's expedition had been unconcerned about what, if any, science had occurred on the journey. The Admiralty in the person of Commander McAllen kept them quiet. Cal wasn't called before a board of inquiry and no one inspected the contents of Sifton's crates.

All this lack of action occurred within a day of her writing her complaint. The response had been blandly insulting, suggesting she was getting too emotional.

She stared out the window of the train. The non-response only supported Sifton. He clearly knew exactly what he was doing. Cal wondered what price she would have paid if she'd waited for him. Probably become his pet Captain, completely tied to him for work carrying him around on his spying trips.

"Lady Shillingsworth," a man she didn't recognize sat beside her. "His Highness told me you prefer Cal." He handed her a tiny scroll. Cal opened it to see a note which read:

This is my man, please hear him out.

It was signed and sealed by the Crown Prince.

"Very well, say your piece." Cal handed the paper back.

"Sometimes in the name of the nation, we must employ unpleasant individuals, because they are good at what they do." He sighed. "Personally, I'd like to take him out and shoot him, but Intelligence needs him. He has come closest to finding what we are looking for."

"So you're asking me to back off and let him destroy my reputation in the name of national pride?" Cal didn't try to keep the bitterness from her voice.

"Not at all." The man smiled, face grim. "We are asking you not to hint he's spying for us. You came dangerously close at Lord Carroway's talking about his cargo." He raised his eyebrow at Cal's face. "Oh yes, we're keeping tabs on him. Dropped a couple of hints about smuggling which is embarrassing, but not a risk to the country. Find a way to take him down a notch which doesn't threaten our national interests, and you'll make a lot of friends in places that matter."

"Thank you. Let his Highness know I understand, and in this as in everything else I am his loyal servant."

The man nodded and slipped away, leaving Cal once again looking out the window. She began making plans. Shifton was easy to anger. From what she saw on board the Kestrel, he loved being in control and manipulating people. Why would someone like that want to face the Gates of Hell?

The only answer Cal could come up with was the man had to prove to everyone he wasn't a coward. She grinned evilly at her reflection. That's why he was so determined to show her a coward, it was the worst thing he could imagine being.

Cal started when the conductor came by announcing her stop. She'd spent the time making plans. She gathered her thoughts and set them aside. No use involving Pentam and Crysabel in her troubles. She'd hardly had a chance to see them between voyages, so nothing was going to spoil this visit.

# Chapter 5  - Old Friends

"I can't believe people are being such fools."
Pentam stormed around the room as Cal and
Crysabel watched, along with the Crysabel's
mother, the Baroness.

"Most people are fools, Dear." Crysabel
sipped at her water. "It is what allows them to
survive the ultimate boredom of their lives."

Pentam stopped and looked at her in shock.

"Think about it. What do these people do?
They wouldn't be caught dead working, they might
dabble in supporting a business venture, but aside
from gossip their lives are meaningless. They are
more to be pitied."

"Not all of them." The Baroness frowned
slightly. "There are many who are involved in
charity works and other worthy causes."

"Very true, Mother, and those people are least likely to be swayed by the scandal of the day."

"Either way," Cal said, meeting Pentam's gaze. "I do not want to spend my visit talking of such matters."

"You're right." Pentam sat down and rubbed his eyes. "I'm just upset because there is nothing I can do."

"You don't need to do anything." Cal moved her shoulders to get rid of the tension in her neck. "You have your thesis and your family to think about. I will be fine."

Pentam looked at her doubtfully, so Cal pulled out a sketchbook.

"Let me show you a bit of our trip." They spent time until dinner looking at her drawings.

"I'd like to see a drawing of the Gates of Hell." Pentam closed the book and handed it to Cal. "It would be hugely popular given their reputation."

"Perhaps I will try again while I'm here." Cal stared out the window. "I haven't been able to capture the ferocity of the place."

"If I know you, a drawing you think to be second-rate will stun anyone else." Crysabel pointed at her. "You're too hard on yourself sometimes. Not everything needs to be perfect."

"Come, it is time to eat." The Baroness led them to the dining room.

That evening Cal sat in her room with her sketchbook open in front of her. The few attempts she'd made at the Gates of Hell felt flat and lifeless. She closed her eyes and tried to capture her feelings as she'd steered through the immense waves. Fear for her ship and her crew. The smallness of the Kestrel in the face of the titanic clash of oceans. Exhilaration at the challenge. Her hand moved on its own...when it stopped she opened her eyes and gasped. The lines on the paper jumped out at her, angry and dangerous. The sky in the east was growing light when Cal finally put down her pencil and stepped back to look at her creation.

Dark with bits of white where froth blew off the water, or waves crashed together. A tiny ship braved the tempestuous ocean with mountainous swells all around. Waves sloshed over the bow making it look as if it were on the point of sinking.

Cal set it aside and collapsed on her bed. She could get a few hours' sleep before the house awoke.

***

"This is amazing!" Crysabel looked mesmerized by Cal's drawing. "That little ship looks so brave."

"This would be a stunning engraving." Pentam rubbed his chin. "I know a fellow who is always desperate for money for plates and such. He's very good. I bet he could do something with this, in return for some help with costs."

"How about I leave it in your hands." Cal rolled the paper and handed it to Pentam.

"It sounds like you don't like it." Crysabel put her hand on Cal's arm.

"It's not that... but looking back, I should never have been there. I didn't know enough to say no, and lost a good man because of it."

"There's a story going around the taverns at the port about a Captain who pulled off a rescue in the middle of this." Pentam waved the tube. "You wouldn't know anything about it would you?"

Cal felt the heat rise on her face.

"For more than one reason, I should have let him drown." She sighed and stretched. "What's done is done, and I won't be making that mistake again."

"How is rescuing someone a mistake?" Pentam asked.

"When it risks the ship and crew. It is only luck we didn't capsize or break apart. The old girl is tougher than she looks." Cal shook herself. "I have something else I wanted to ask about." She pulled out a sketchbook and opened it to the drawings of the machine from the Dynasty.

"What is it?" Pentam peered at the drawing.

"I have no idea other than it has something to do with electricity. The rumours were someone in the Zithayan Dynasty found a way to produce lightning on-demand."

"It's not a battery. There are no moving parts, and this looks like a coil. Maybe copper wire?"

"How would it work?" Crysabel moved around to look.

"A battery is a chemical reaction which creates a current through a copper wire. Think of a spark as energy jumping from one place to another. The greater the distance, the more energy required." Pentam dipped his finger in Crysabel's water and she stuck her tongue out at him. He held his hand so the water formed a drop on the tip of his finger. "It builds up until it has enough to leap." The droplet fell. "Then it starts building again. A battery creates a steady stream of drops. This would do the same thing from what you said. Interesting, but I'm not sure about its usefulness."

"Enough people think it important that some died for this picture." Cal handed the book to Pentam. "I burned the original, then tried to recreate it from memory. Don't tell anyone about this. I mean it, not a soul! Please, see if you can figure it out, Pentam."

Pentam looked through the book again.

"Don't let it stop you from working on your thesis." Crysabel wagged a finger at Pentam.

"I'm studying the effect of acid on some metals, so I've built a battery since it involved metal and acid. I can fit this in." He stood up and wandered away, deep in thought.

"Oh well," Cal said, "but now you can tell me all about this baby without embarrassing him."

***

After a few very enjoyable days, Cal reluctantly boarded the train to go home. Once again she spent most of the trip staring out the window. A reflection caught her attention. How many times had the same person walked past her seat? Sifton's sneering face came to mind. She wouldn't put it past him to have her followed to get more ammunition.

Cal disembarked and carried her bag and satchel as usual. Ship life had taught her to pack light, and since she and Crysabel were the same size, Cal hadn't packed any gowns. She hailed a cab and headed for home, watching out the window to see if someone jumped out to follow her. No one did. So either she was imagining things, or they knew where she was going and had people there.

She pulled a sheet of paper from her satchel and wrote a quick note, folded and sealed it.

"I need to go by the post office." She called up to the cabbie. He pulled up in front of the building a few minutes later.

"Wait for me, I'll only be a moment." Cal walked up the steps. It didn't take long to buy a stamp and mail her letter. The cab took her the rest of the way home and she gave him a large tip.

"Hello, Beth." Cal greeted the cook and housekeeper. "How were things while I was gone?"

"Oh dear." Beth wrung her hands. "The master..." She wiped at a tear. "He got angry and tried to throw me out of the house. Said he'd never hired any servants. Then the next minute he was discussing dinner as if nothing had happened. He's been in his study ever since, and I can't get a word out of him."

Cal handed off her bags. "I'll go talk to him right away." She almost ran to her father's office, knocked on the door and walked in.

"Oh hello, Meredith. Time for tea already? I'm sorry I forgot the time." He fumbled through his papers. "Where did I put my watch?"

Cal's stomach sank and she had to fight back tears.

"Father, it's Calliope."

He stopped fumbling and looked up at her.

"Of course you are, what was I thinking? Comes from reading too many old journals. Well, let's go for tea, shall we?"

"You go ahead and wash up, I'll be right there."

Sir Shillingsworth picked up a cane and limped out of the room.

When did he start using a cane again? What's going on? Cal walked around the desk and sifted through the papers. They were a mishmash of journals, drawings and invoices. The leather-bound book where her father had been recording his life was closed, with a leather marker part way through. She opened the book to the marker. The pages were filled with nonsense, not even letters anymore as though he'd forgotten how to write.

Cal collapse in her father's chair. What had happened to her father? Where had the brilliant man she'd grown up with gone? Cal fought back tears, they certainly wouldn't help. She wasn't sure anything would.

***

Cal left in the morning in the steam carriage and headed to the university. Once there she asked directions to Professor Orthin's office.

"Cal, I'd heard you were home. What a delight! You must tell me all about your adventures." The smile left his face as Cal struggled to fight back tears. Facing the Gates wasn't a terrifying as this.

"It's Father," she said and burst into tears.

After several cups of tea, Cal was able to tell the Professor about her concerns, interrupted by the occasional hiccup.

"I see..." Professor Orthin sat back and stared up at the ceiling. "There are a few things which would cause what you're describing, none of them good. I know an excellent doctor you can trust. Why don't you invite me for supper this evening and I will bring him along. He owes me a favour or two."

"Thank you." Cal cut off her words before she began sobbing again.

Cal went home to tell Beth they'd be having guests for supper.

"Miss, could you call your father. He's late for lunch. Maybe he'll listen to you." Beth twisted her apron in her hands.

"Right away." Cal knocked on the door of Sir Shillingsworth's office then walked in. He sat slumped over his papers.

"Father?" He looked like he was sleeping. He had been more tired the last couple of days. Cal walked around the desk and shook him. Sir Shillingsworth fell out of the chair. Cal tried to catch him and ended up on the floor with her father on her legs. His face looked up at her, but his eyes were clouded. His hand cold in hers.

Cal was a child again going in to wake her mother, only to find her dead. Now as then, she screamed and screamed until Beth and Hans dragged her away so they could take care of her father.

***

The church was filled with people. Pentam and Crysabel sat on one side of Cal, Beth and Hans on the other. She'd said her final goodbye and had no intentions of getting up until it was time to take him to the cemetery. Distinguished scientists, one after another, droned on about the contributions Sir Shillingsworth had made to science.

Cal fought back tears. None of them knew him, not really. Impulsively, Cal stood and walked to the lectern where Dr. Franklyn was speaking. He stopped in mid-sentence and ushered her into place, then stood beside her.

She stared out at the crowd, so many people. What did she think she could say to them?

"He was my father." Once the words started, she couldn't stop or control them. "He adored my mother. Whenever he got home from a trip the two of them would grin and bump into each other for days. I was too young to understand but never forgave himself for not being there when she died. Soon afterwards, I started drawing for him. We talked about it just the other day, he had the first sketch I ever did on one of his expeditions," she brushed away her tears. "On his last voyage, I got to go along and see what he did. I got to know him better on that one trip than I ever did before. He stayed home after that, saying he was writing his memoirs. From then on, I became the one who travelled." Cal looked down at Dr. Franklyn's careful notes, and her control shattered. Tears ran down her face. "I thought I'd have more time with him."

Dr. Franklyn helped her back to her seat where Crysabel put her arms around Cal's shoulders as they both sobbed.

The service wrapped up quickly and it was time to go to the cemetery. Cal walked with Pentam and Hans supporting her from either side.

While the service felt like it had taken forever, the graveside prayers were over too soon. Cal didn't want to leave. People on the fringes of the crowd wandered away, but many stayed to support her.

"Goodbye, Father. At least you and Mother are together again. You can tell her all about our adventure. Thank you."

"It is so sad you didn't have more time with the old man." Lord Sifton stood to one side, his face blank of emotion. "But at least he was spared the embarrassment of his daughter losing her command."

Pentam stepped forward but Cal beat him to it.

"You snivelling coward. What are you proving by sneering at a grieving daughter? I talked to the Naval Academy about my command, and the only thing they were concerned about was the fact I stopped to rescue you. If I was the hopeless case you'd like people to believe I am, you would be dead and gone in Hell with not one person sorrier for it. Maybe that's why you aren't bragging about staring the Gates in the eye and spitting because it would force you to admit this ship captain has more decency and courage than someone like you could ever aspire to!"

Lord Sifton's lips curled when Cal started speaking, but they thinned as his face paled. Her father's dead eyes had held more warmth than the glare Sifton gave her. He opened his mouth, but several men stepped in front of him and not very gently hauled him away.

"Naval officers, come to pay their respects." Commander McAllen kept his face amiable, but Cal saw the fire burning in his eyes. "They don't take kindly to folks harassing grieving women. But he's a bad person to have as an enemy."

"So am I," Cal said.

# Chapter 6  - A new thing

Cal would have shut up the house and moved into rooms in the city, except it would have left Beth and Hans with nowhere to go.

"Surely somewhere there are people who need a place to stay." Cal sat in the kitchen while Beth kneaded bread. "I rattle around here, it's ridiculous."

"I understand there are usually University students looking for a residence. My sister works there as a cleaner. She would ask if you'd like."

"I would like that. A few students would bring some life here, and maybe they could help with organizing father's papers."

"Then I will ask."

Within the week the first student arrived. He looked shocked to have a bedroom to himself with a desk and chair. When Cal went to check on him before she went to bed, he'd covered every flat surface with paper. He flitted from one to another.

"Oh, hello, Miss Shillingsworth. Pray, pardon the disarray," he waved distractedly at the piles. "I have an upcoming exam and all my notes were mixed up in the move."

"If you need more space, you could use the drawing room for an afternoon. It has the most tables."

"No, no, I'm good now. I can't possibly move them again." He shuddered, then looked at the bed. "Guess I'm sleeping on the floor tonight."

"Breakfast begins at seven." Cal left him to his study and went to her rooms.

More students arrived and filled the house with chatter and laughter. It didn't feel like her home anymore and Cal sighed in relief.

Bundo arrived one morning a week later with a bag and a wide grin. He handed Cal a sheaf of papers extending her leave until she was ready to return, then followed Hans into the stable to find a room to stay in.

"We want people to think I'm your servant you brought back. Many officers do exactly that. If I live in the stable no one will give me a second thought, and no one will see me come and go."

"As you wish," Cal said but promised herself he'd get a proper bed.

That evening Cal pulled Hans aside.

"I want you to look at a drawing for me." She unrolled a large paper and anchored the corners with books. "This is a plan for fixing up the barn; with everything going on in the house, it seems a waste to leave it empty."

"That's all well and good." Hans pointed to posts along the long walls. "What are these? The stone doesn't need reinforcing.

"That's so I can open the roof." Cal laughed at Hans' expression. "I'm trying to build an airship. I will need a way to get it in and out of the barn. Those pillars are actually metal tubes filled with oil. It's under pressure so they stay extended. Release the pressure, they sink down and the roof follows on a track." She indicated the pertinent points on the blueprint as she spoke. "There's space under the barn to build everything I need. The floor needs replacing anyway."

"Who's going to do all the work?" Hans peered at the drawing again. "None of this will be cheap."

"I'm not exactly poor." Cal felt the heat on her face. "Father was as proficient an investor as he was a leader. I never need to worry about money for the rest of my life. And once I prove it works, I can sell it to the Navy."

"So they can launch their ships through the roof."

"Exactly."

"I'll get some people in to look at the place and start clearing out rubble."

The students decided rebuilding the barn was a great diversion. At any time during the day, a few were to be found with shovels and wheelbarrows working under Hans' sharp-eyed supervision.

***

A letter came from the expedition company ordering Cal to return to command the Kestrel on a new voyage.

"Come along with me, Bundo." Cal checked out the steam carriage, decided it would survive the trip and lit the fire.

He nodded. "I will pack."

"No need. We'll be back tonight."

Cal drove the carriage to the port. It wasn't much faster than the train, but much more convenient. She parked in front of the Expedition Offices.

"Let's go." Cal squared her shoulders and walked through the doors.

"Ah, Captain. You made better time than I'd hoped." Mister Hacket was a retired captain, heavy-set but he still looked like he could clear out a tavern single-handed.

"Sorry, Mister Hacket, but I'm here to resign my command."

"Surely you aren't letting that worm, Sifton get to you? Henrichs said you were a fine Captain."

"Thank you, but I have other work I must do."

"It's an awful shame to lose you, Lady Shillingsworth. Would you consider taking an indefinite leave?" He suggested, eyebrows raised hopefully.

"Sorry, but I will not be back."

"You'll want to collect your things from the Kestrel then. You know where she is berthed." He looked over at Bundo. "Am I right in guessing this fine gentleman is now under your employ?"

"Yes, Sir."

"You don't need me to tell you to take care of Lady Shillingsworth."

"No, Sir. Thank you for the chance to work on your ship. Not everyone would have hired me."

"Nonsense. You're a good man and a good sailor. Doesn't matter where you're from."

Cal and Bundo signed the necessary papers, then she drove down to the dock.

"Permission to come aboard?" She called from the bottom of the gangway.

"What do you mean?" Paul came to the rail. "She's your ship."

"Not anymore." Cal pushed back the tears threatening to fall.

"Well then, permission granted." Paul met her at the top of the ramp. "I'm guessing you need your gear from your cabin. You know where it is."

Cal and Bundo packed up her clothes and the little rug in a duffle; it didn't take much time. She put sketchbooks in her satchel. The bottle of brandy from Captain Jenkins was still a quarter full. Cal picked it up, while Bundo shouldered the duffle and they returned to the deck.

"Captain." Paul stood at attention along with Joliu and Jorges. "I will call you Captain one last time," he asserted when she attempted to demur. He saluted her along with the others. Wherever you go, know the Kestrel and her crew will come if you call."

Cal returned their salute, then handed Paul the bottle.

"Drink this as a toast for me. I've said it before, but I'll say it again. You are the best-damned crew afloat."

She walked down the gangway and didn't look back.

****

The day after they'd returned to the city, Bundo drove Cal to the Naval Academy. He'd decided driving was a necessary skill to protect her, so Hans had taught him. He picked up driving as quickly as he had the duties of purser on the Kestrel.

"I don't know how long I'll be, so you might as well head home. I'll hire a cab."

"I'll wait." Bundo pointed across the yard to where a tree offered shade. "You live as if you are safe. I will live as if you are not."

"Very well. I can hardly hire you, then ignore your advice." Cal waved at him and climbed the steps to the imposing door. Guards in dress uniform stood on either side of the door, but she noted the worn hilts on their swords and the freshly oiled metal on their rifles. One of them nodded slightly to her as she stepped through the door.

She'd considered wearing her captain's uniform, but since she'd effectively resigned, it didn't feel right. The plain, tailored dress would have to do in its place. The only accent was the gold Royal Engineer pin the Crown Prince had given her.

The atrium echoed with voices, sounding like surf on the shore. Cal looked around for a logical person to speak to and spotted an older man sitting behind a desk. The worn heels of her boots tapped out a staccato rhythm as she walked across the marble floor, lavishly inset with a compass rose in the centre. The ceiling had a scene painted on it, but she wasn't about to stop and admire it.

"I was asked to stop in at the Naval Academy."

"What's your business, so I can direct you properly." The man looked up at Cal.

"I'm not sure. Captain Jenkins told me to come. He wrote a letter for me." She handed it to the man, who looked at it with wide eyes.

"I see." He stood up. "Follow me."

They walked along a hallway with paintings of ships in all kinds of weather. One caught Cal's eye.

"I didn't know anyone had done a painting of The Gates of Hell."

"HMSS Oberon. First Navy ship to travel through the Gates. When Captain Abrams retired, he took up painting. That's one of his."

"It's very good. He's captured the feel of the Gates." Cal pointed to the ship cresting a wave, water pouring off the deck. "We had a hard enough time with a steamship. I can't imagine passing through them under sail."

"Captain Abrams wrote a very descriptive passage in the ship's log. All officers in training are required to read it. He lost five men and very nearly sank more than once. His comments summarize the pain of losing men under one's command."

"It is painful beyond measure to find your imagined invulnerability doesn't extend to the men in your command. A healthy fear of death may save more than one."

"You've read the passage?" The man looked at her with renewed interest.

"A plaque on the bridge of a ship I didn't understand until too late." Cal put her hand on her heart and breathed slowly until the tide of guilt subsided.

"Come." The man turned away and walked along the hall to the first double doors. A guard stood outside them.

"He's got a few minutes free before the Admiralty meets. It's rumoured Himself is planning to be there so it will be a tough one."

"Thanks for the warning." Cal's guide held up Captain Jenkins' letter. "He'll want to see this one."

"Very well." The guard opened the door and announced them. "Chief Petty Officer Gallahad, with a guest. He says you will want to meet her."

"Fascinating." The baritone voice could have rattled the doors on their hinges. Cal got the impression the speaker constantly restrained its power. "By all means send them in."

Cal followed the Chief Petty Officer into a room which made her stop dead in shock. She'd expected more art, wood panelling, even luxurious furniture, but the large room was sparsely decorated and what furniture it contained was utilitarian. While she examined the room, her guide handed the letter to a man behind a large desk. He turned and left the room, giving Cal a slight nod on the way past. She shook her head and approached the desk. The man wore a working uniform as plain as his office, but his insignia indicated he held a high rank.

The man frowned slightly as he read Captain Jenkins' letter. Cal stood patiently waiting for him to finish.

"Why didn't you sit?" He put the letter on his desk.

"I wouldn't take a seat on a Captain's bridge without his permission."

"I think I see what Captain Jenkins was talking about." He waved at a chair. "Take a seat. Did Gallahad tell you whom he was taking you to see?"

"No, Sir."

"Figures. He didn't want you too nervous to talk. Vice-Admiral Peysk."

"Calliope Shillingsworth."

"Not Captain?" The Vice-Admiral raised an eyebrow.

"Not any longer. There is work I need to do which can't be managed aboard a ship. I hope someday to command a ship again."

"Tell me about this work that took you away from the sea." He leaned back, fingers playing with a button on his jacket.

"Almost two years ago, His Highness the Crown Prince asked me to build him an airship. He told me to learn something about command first. So I spent a year and a half as First Mate on the Kestrel, and the last voyage as Captain."

"His Highness asked you?" The eyebrow went up higher this time.

"At the same time, he gave me this." Cal handed him the scroll detailing her role as Royal Engineer. The Vice-Admiral read the scroll looking more and more shocked.

"That's just like Himself to create an entirely new branch of the Navy, and fail to inform anyone of his actions." He picked up the letter and handed the scroll back to Cal. Coming around the desk he peered at the pin on her blouse. "I see. Understated but very clear." He headed for the door. "Well come along. Don't want to keep the Admiralty waiting."

Cal jogged to catch up to him, then had to walk fast to stay beside him. The Vice-Admiral opened a door and ushered Cal through before closing the door behind him. She'd never seen so much gold braid in one place, but all the men stood immediately.

"They don't stand that quickly for me. Maybe I should try wearing a dress." The Crown Prince stepped over to her and took her hand. "I've been waiting for you to show up. You wouldn't believe the mess we're dealing with." He guided her to a seat.

"Would you care to explain just who she is and what she has to do with the present situation?" One of the men spoke gruffly.

"Certainly." The Crown Prince brought Cal to a chair at the table. "Please sit, gentlemen." The six men lowered themselves into their seats as the prince dropped into his seat and sighed happily. "Meet Lady Calliope Shillingsworth, who prefers to be called Cal." He winked at her. "Cal is a very talented artist, and more to the point has an innate understanding of engines and machinery. That landing tower which caused you so much grief until I passed on a suggestion? The solution was Cal's—tossed out within seconds of hearing the problem. She even proposed an alternative, but it would have had the builders pulling out their hair. She also asked all the pertinent questions about how an airship would work, just from seeing one for the first time. Questions mind you, that not one of your Navy engineers asked. Given her ability, I appointed her as my first Royal Engineer but asked her to get some experience with command. She's going to need it."

"What do you mean 'I'm going to need it? I thought you wanted me to build you an airship?" Cal burst out.

"We have engineers," the Prince said, "and they are very good at building ships to float on the ocean. We have the best fleet in the world because of those engineers. But someone is going to have to convince them to think differently to build an airship." The prince pointed at her.

"Since his Royal Highness casually created a new branch of the navy, dedicated solely to engineering new machines." Vice-Admiral Peysk grinned at Cal. "There is no existing command structure—outside of yourself, that is. Naturally, as a commander of a branch of our Royal Navy, you will be expected to report to this group."

"I hadn't thought of that." The prince rubbed his chin. "But it's a good idea. Complete secrecy will be impossible with a project this big, but if we can keep as much of the detail in this room as possible, it would help."

Cal closed her mouth with a snap.

"Admiral Shillingsworth. Has a nice ring to it." The Vice-Admiral grinned at her.

"You are not making me an Admiral." Cal put her hands flat on the table to stop them shaking. "Royal Engineer is rarified enough."

"What is the command structure for engineers now?" One of the Admirals asked.

"Not sure there is one. They are under whichever branch enlisted them, and their rank comes from that branch. If we're to combine them into their own branch, we'll need to create an entirely new chain of command." The Vice-Admiral looked up at the ceiling. "What we don't want is her getting bogged down in the paperwork instead of building our airship. I suggest we have an administrative office to manage the paperwork and give our Royal Engineer a working rank. Chief Engineer sounds too much like Chief Petty Officer, so maybe something like Commander of the Royal Engineers? Her duties won't be far off what a Commander does now, and we can adjust as we go along."

"Works for me." The prince looked around the table as the Admirals nodded. "That's out of the way. I'll let you and Cal work out the details later. What I want to hear now, is how we're going to build this thing."

"I've been giving it considerable thought." Cal wished she'd known what the meeting was about. Then she could have brought her sketchbook with her drawings and notes. "I have some preliminary drawings, but before we start putting things together I need to learn some important things. First, is what volume we need to displace to float an airship. Second, we need to look at different ways of creating the volume. Hot air will lift a weight from the ground, and hot air balloons have been around for a while. The problem is how we heat the necessary amount of air and keep it hot.

There may be other solutions to make a lighter-than-air volume. We'll explore them. Third, we need an engine, a propeller for it to drive and a mechanism to steer both port and starboard as well as up and down."

The prince held up his hand to forestall her as the Admiral stared at her with glazed eyes. "Thank you, Commander. What resources do you need?"

"People who won't mind working with a woman. I don't have time to coddle men who want to push me around because of who I am. I also need the biggest open building you have. Even a prototype airship is going to be huge." She drummed her fingers on the heavy, mahogany table. "A full machine shop and people to run it, preferably creative people. And I will need silk or some similar lightweight fabric. Canvas will be too heavy. Everything we make for this ship will need to be light and efficient."

"Just how much silk are we talking? My wife bought a silk dress and it cost a small fortune." One of the Admirals waved his hands in the air.

"I may be able to find another fabric which will work, but that's a priority."

"Very well. Keep us informed." The prince steepled his fingers. "Now, I know we have some other business."

"Excuse me, with all due respect. I don't have the experience to contribute to your other discussion. Since I've made my report, I would like to return to my work."

"Return to your work? You haven't even started yet. We need to swear you in and get you oriented." Vice-Admiral Peysk looked shocked.

"I need to design experiments to learn more of the parameters I'm working with. I also need to work on the engine and steering component design."

"How about we swear her in now, and do it all officially later?" The Crown Prince said, looking at the others.

"That's what you said when you made me Royal Engineer."

"I did, didn't I?" He grinned at her, not the least bit apologetic. "Well, I'll work on that. For the moment, do you swear..."

# Chapter 7  - Royal Engineers

Cal turned in a circle to take in the dusky space.

"They call it the Shed. No one remembers why this thing was built, but it is the biggest enclosed space available." Commander McAllen pointed to one wall. "All along there are rooms of various sizes from broom closets to meeting rooms for fifty people. Above them is an open gallery to observe the main space." He headed up the stairs. "This room at the end has a special treat." He pushed open a panel in the wall to reveal a short hallway to more stairs. "These bypass the gallery and go to the roof." Another door let them out onto a flat section of roof with a small barn-sized building.

"I think at one time they had cadets rappelling down the wall. There are still harnesses and ropes in the barn, though I'd hate to have to use one after all this time."

"I'm not sure we want people up here just yet." Cal stood a safe distance from the edge of the roof. "With the wind, it's too risky, and it isn't likely the engineers will need to learn to rappel."

"Not the engineers perhaps, but once we have airships, the crew will need to know how to use ropes to get to the ground."

Cal frowned thoughtfully. He made a good point.

"If you can arrange for me to learn, it would help in designing the airship. We will need hatches in the floor, places to store and anchor ropes, a way to bring the ropes and people back up into the airship, all things I hadn't thought of yet."

"Consider it done. There is a climbing and rappelling wall on the other side of the Academy. There's always a group working on it."

They returned down the stairs to the room. McAllen pulled the panel open to let them back into the room.

"Spring loaded for some reason." He shrugged.

Cal rubbed dirt off the glass and looked out the window. "How many rooms have windows like this?"

"The biggest room does, and this one."

"I'll make this my office; the light will be best in here." Cal walked around the space. "I'll need a table by the window and another along this wall. Shelves to organize books and papers along the wall with the panel. Put a desk by the panel. Chairs for each table."

"If you think of anything else let me know."

They walked through all the rooms with Cal deciding on their purpose. The administrative office would be next door to hers. The largest room set up as a mess and for large meetings. Other rooms for storage or small-scale experiments.

Cal found the stairs to the gallery and leaned on the rail. She imagined the shop as she pointed to different areas. "We'll want to keep the centre of the space open, but we'll need a foundry and machine shop; maybe in the corner by the big doors to make deliveries easier. Tool storage along the wall. I'm sure there will be other needs we discover as we go." If she had her way they would start this instant but she reined back her enthusiasm. Didn't want to miss something important. "The first thing will be building a steam supply near the foundry. A wall for safety when we're testing engine prototypes."

"How big a wall?"

"You ever see a boiler explode?" she asked dryly.

"Right, big and strong." McAllen led the way back to the ground. "I'll have a crew in clearing out and cleaning tomorrow. It will be ready for you within the week."

"I'll be here tomorrow; there may be surprises or useful items."

"If you're here, I have a security detail for you."

"Okay, but I have my own man whom they will need to coordinate with."  Her lips twitched at the thought of telling Bundo he was going to have company.

"Great, I'll see you tomorrow."

***

By the end of the week, the building shone. A boiler had been set up with a chimney to the outside. A foundry and forge sat next to it, also vented outside. The safety wall had been constructed from oak planks and attached to the wall with beams. Upstairs, furniture filled the rooms.

The day they "opened for business," so to speak, Cal stood in the huge open expanse and listened as Commander McAllen explained security procedures. The men were all Navy and knew the drill. When he'd finished, she examined the team of engineers. The twelve men looked back at her doubtfully.

"I am Commander Cal Shillingsworth of the Royal Engineers. Team leaders will report to me. For now, we will have a team working on boiler design, another on engine design, and one to determine what displacement we need to lift the ship. As we progress, I will create new teams to take on tasks as they come up.

"You are here because your commanding officer recommended you for your engineering ability, but also your willingness to be creative in finding solutions. I don't want to spend all my time telling you what to do. Come up with a plan, execute it, evaluate, and adjust the plan. Any questions you may have, bring to me only after you've kicked them around."

"Why are you here?" A sandy-haired man stepped forward, his arms crossed.

"Name please."

"Petty Officer Johns, Ma'am."

"Thank you, we'll keep the formalities to a minimum so they don't interfere with our work. Call me Commander. In an emergency yell 'Cal'. As to why I'm here, his Highness the Crown Prince

Hurbert appointed me. If you have a problem with that, take it up with him. My job is to ask questions which you will then find answers for."

"How are you going to determine the teams and team leaders? Ensign Cesare, Commander."  A second man addressed her.

"You know what you're good at better than I. Your dossiers are on my desk and I will be reviewing them, but for now I want you to divide yourselves. Team leader will be the highest rank on the team, for now. I want five each on boiler and engine, and two for the displacement work. Those two will eventually lead the design of the envelope."

"Why don't we just build a ship like the Ferandicans? Engineer Second Class Digney."

"Good question. First, the Ferandicans haven't shared their design with us. As allies, it would be in poor taste to steal it. Second, their ship is great in calm weather but struggles in any kind of wind. We need an all-weather craft. Third, because we are going to build the best airship in the world, and we can't do that by starting with someone else's ideas. The better we understand the principles of airships, the better we can make ours work. Now, enough talk. Divide yourselves into teams, then team leaders come and see me in my office upstairs. It will be the one with me working in it." Cal saluted them, then headed to her office.

A man in immaculate uniform waited for her.

"Chief Petty Officer O'Brien." He stood up as she came in. "I will be managing your security."

"Thank you, I have a man who will be guarding me while I'm off-site. You and your detail will take care of when I'm at the Academy. If you have any concerns, you will bring them to me immediately. Aside from that, let your men know to obey safety instructions from any of the engineers. I have no intention of losing anyone to accidents."

"Yes, Commander. I will bring them to introduce you tomorrow."

"Excellent. Dismissed." Cal pulled paper over and began sketching out ideas. A knock on the door interrupted her.

"Excuse me, Commander. I'm Petty Officer Tallinan; I'll be your purser and manage the administrative side of things. Commander McAllen has briefed me. As your team grows, I'm afraid I'll need to bring in assistants."

"Pleased to meet you. I've set aside an office for you next door. If you need anything, bring me the requisition."

Ensign Cesare entered as Tallinan left.

"I've been made team lead for the two of us working on the envelope. You said something about displacement?"

"Yes. The purpose of the envelope will be to displace enough air to make the ship float. We will need something lighter than air to fill the envelope. I'm told hydrogen is cheapest and most plentiful."

"Dangerous, too, not sure I'd want to sail on a firetrap."

"Part of your work will be making the envelope as fireproof as possible, but first we must determine how much a cubic foot of hydrogen will lift. That will give us the size of the envelope and the maximum weight of the craft. I don't trust the numbers I've been seeing, there's too much variance."

"We'll need a supply of hydrogen, and balloons to fill. I'll check with the purser."

"Good, let me know when you're ready to start testing."

"Aye, Commander."

Digney entered next.

"What do you have in mind for the boiler?" He scanned the room and visibly relaxed. Keeping the room obviously about work was the right move.

"The weight of the water and boiler may be the single heaviest part of the ship. To give the ship range we'll either need a large boiler to supply steam or a smaller boiler at higher pressure. The large boiler isn't a problem; we can lift one from any ship or train. I'd like to focus on creating the highest pressure possible. I'm thinking a sphere, but I'm open to suggestions. You'll need to design boilers, then test at what pressure they fail. You have the space behind the plank wall to use."

"I recommend we start with small models and work up. The pressures won't be identical, but it will be a good start. Layers of steel may be the best bet, but one of the guys is looking into other materials to reinforce it."

"Sounds good. I will expect you to produce a safety protocol for testing. I'll tolerate no injuries from carelessness."

"Aye Commander. I will have something for you by the end of the day."

The last team leader was a grizzled man with a scar across his cheek.

"Engineer First Class Landers. My team and I've already had an argument about the engine. One of the fellows insists the piston engine won't give enough power. The screw will need to be bigger and turn faster than in the water. We'll blow up a couple of engines testing his theory, but first, we need to know the shape of the screw. So with your permission, we will start there."

"Good thinking. Carry on."

Cal went to look out the window. She itched to be down messing about with the teams but proving she trusted them to do the work was more important. Birds flew past, their wings a blur for the small ones, the larger birds gliding on wings held rigidly. Too bad they couldn't fly like a bird, but she had no idea how they could copy the flapping wings. Cal watched the gulls glide on the wind a bit longer, then went to her desk and began sketching.

***

Over the following weeks, Cesare and his team used carefully constructed balloons to measure the lift of hot air versus hydrogen. They quickly determined hot air wouldn't be enough to float the airship. Even with hydrogen, they needed an enormous volume to lift a small weight. Armed with that information, Cal worked through her plans, cutting weight everywhere she could.

The boiler would be the biggest challenge. Train engines operated at much higher pressures than steamships, but to drive the airship any distance even they would be too heavy. The team struggled with spherical tanks as flaws in the shape became catastrophic much quicker than with cylinders. Cal started every time a boiler blew. Even the small prototypes made a considerable bang. She finally asked them to give her a five-minute warning so she wouldn't spoil so many drawings. Since her work paused for the time of the test, she began watching from the gallery. Even as her team's manufacturing skills improved, the balls failed where the two hemispheres joined. Cal headed down to listen in on their evaluation.

"Don't matter what we do with the flange, it blows. We can't tighten it enough."

"What about putting a lip inside the flange on one side?"

"Could do, I guess. I still think the issue is the join."

"We tried welds and we've tried bolting it, don't think a bit of a lip will help."

"What if you nested spheres, and staggered where the joins were?" Cal scratched her head. Then used a bit of chalk to illustrate on a convenient patch of blank wall. "See?  Each layer reinforces the others. If we wrap in between layers with something with no give it would even out any spaces between the layers. We might be able to use a smaller amount of steel in total as a result."

"Hmmm," Digney peered at her scratches on the wall. "Worth trying. We'd want to set the fittings in each layer, or they'll blow. Need a new design for valves to handle the pressure. If we set the valve in the boiler, we won't have to fuss with the output pipe."

The others nodded and started discussing details and how to test them. Cal winked at Digney and went back to work.

She passed the room where Landers and his group had set up fans with different shaped blades to measure which was most efficient.

"Commander?" The old engineer called Cal in. "We're leaning toward this design. We have doubled up two oak props. Need a lot more surface than the water propellers to push the air. We found longer was better than wider. Four blades work best."

"Good work. I'm thinking you'll need the engine to test how fast they can spin before failing."

"That would be our next step. We'll start with a standard engine, least we know how to build 'em. A couple of us are working on something which will spin the shaft directly."

"Interesting. How do they plan on doing that?"

"Patrick wondered if a fan could push air if air could push a fan. Not as simple as all that, but he's been lying awake at night thinking about it."

"I'd like to hear more about his ideas." Cal closed her eyes to picture how it might work. It would take a lot of work to make it efficient.

"Commander?" A young man stood at attention in front of her, his knees visibly shaking.

"Sorry, Patrick. I was envisioning your concept." She smiled. "Do you have any drawings?"

"Let me fetch them."

"Bring them to my office, I'll put on tea. Anyone else who wants to kick it around can join us."

In the end Patrick, Landers and Cal sat at a table, tea cups holding his drawing open on the table.

"I see you have the blades enclosed, that's good, but a cylinder might not be the best shape. Remember the steam is under pressure, so it expands as it moves."

"Of course, that's the point."

Landers glared at the young man, but Cal shook her head and he didn't say anything.

"What if we used the expansion to push the fan faster?" Cal sketched a cone with a series of ever larger fans.

"The steam will blow past and we won't get much push." Landers peered at the drawing.

"What if the only path for the steam was past the blades?" Patrick drew a spiral shape with the blades growing larger, set with the cone. "We'll need to figure what shape cone is best and how many blades, but there is no reason we can't drive a shaft with this."

"Okay, Patrick what do you need to build this thing?" The young man looked at Landers, who laughed and slapped the younger man's shoulder.

"It's your project, you do the thinking." Landers nodded at Cal. "We'll need more people, and specialized fabricators would help. I can throw something together, but this will require accuracy beyond my talent."

"Bring me a plan by morning." Cal took a sip of her tea, then pushed the paper back into place. "My gut is telling me this could be a huge jump forward if we can make it work." She met Patrick and Landers' eyes. "Don't talk about this outside of the teams. I've never heard of anything like this, so as of this moment it is secret."

"Aye, Commander." The two men looked at Patrick's drawing with new respect.

***

Outside the Shed, Cal met Commander McAllen riding a horse, holding the reins of a second.

"The climbing wall is a fair distance, don't want you too tired to climb, and coming back here will be worse."

"I used to ride a little with my governess." Cal introduced herself to the horse. "Come on handsome, let's see how much I remember." Mounting in her pants and blouse was much easier than the riding dress her governess insisted she wore. She settled herself in the saddle and picked up the reins.

"We will be working to improve your riding as we go." McAllen set his horse into a trot and Cal followed suit.

"A Navy officer riding a horse?" Cal found the rhythm and settled into it. Her legs were going to complain.

McAllen slowed to a walk. "There are tales of ships so big the captain rode a horse from one end to the other." He laughed at Cal's eye roll. "No skill is ever wasted."

After a pleasant ride with him pointing out sights on the way they arrived at a towering wall. It looked even higher than the roof of the Shed.

"This is where we teach the climbing and rappelling. You'll be fine with the clothes you have. No dresses on the wall, don't want to give the men heart trouble." He winked as he turned Cal over to a Petty Officer who towered over her.

"Unfortunately, I won't be able to ride with you every day. The blighters expect me to work, but I have a good man who will instruct you." He waved and rode away.

"I'm told you want to learn to climb and rappel. What do you know about it?"

"Nothing."

"Good enough." The man waved to someone working on a tangle of ropes. "Clarke. Work the Commander through the ropes and knots she needs."

"Aye." This man looked hardly old enough to be in the Navy, but he was an efficient instructor. "Most think you just tie a rope around your waist and set off. It's a good way to get dead." He showed her how to make a harness which wrapped around her waist and between her legs. "When you have this one down, I'll show you how to make a bosun's chair. You can sit in mid-air with no fear of falling."

After an hour working the ropes, tying and untying knots until her fingers blistered, Cal was allowed to try the wall.

She tied her own harness, with Sailor Clarke double-checking her work. She then tied it to a safety rope which ran up to the top of the wall. Petty Officer Danson braced the rope while Clarke pointed out the first few handholds.

"You need to think ahead of where you are, plan what you're going to do next. Some of the stretches will be too far for you. Plan to go around them. You won't make the top today. Don't worry about it. Focus on getting comfortable, find your balance, then think how to move. If you fall, we'll catch you. That's what the rope is for. If you get tired and can't go higher, lean away from the wall and we'll lower you as you walk down the wall."

Cal swallowed and started up. She made it no more than ten feet before she couldn't reach the next handhold. Her foot slipped as she tried to move sideways. The harness caught her. Following Clarke's instructions, she got her feet on the wall and returned to the ground.

"Let me try again."

Petty Officer Danson nodded.

Cal planned her route better and made it past where she'd got stuck the first time. By the time she reached the twenty-foot mark, her arms shook from exertion. She sighed and waved to the ground then leaned back. Walking down the wall was a new experience for her. On the ground, she shook her arms.

"I'd hoped to do better."

Clarke laughed. "No one does as well as they want the first time. You didn't panic, so count it as a success."

Cal arranged to join a class which met early in the morning. She could climb, then go to work at the Shed.

She rode back to the shed and handed the horse off to a man who met her there. He introduced himself as Able-seaman Twost, and informed her that he'd help her with her riding. He nodded when Cal told him she'd need to be at the wall early in the morning, then led the horse away.

***

"The boiler shouldn't have failed so soon." Digney sat in Cal's office a month into their work. "I looked at the pieces." He dropped a twisted chunk of steel on her desk. "See here where it failed, looks like someone ground a groove in the shell.

I'm putting as much of the thing together as I can, but I wouldn't be surprised to see grinds on parts of each layer."

"Manufacturing mistake?" She asked hopefully.

"Not if the grooves line up to make a weak point."

"You're suggesting sabotage." Cal's gut twisted. She couldn't understand the mentality of someone destroying things. "Watch for problems. Keep track of who works on each piece of the boiler. Keep your ears open for someone whose talk is off. I will get O'Brien to check into the background of all the people on the project. It's time we started to take the secrecy of our work seriously. I'd suggest you paint each layer of new boilers a different colour, it will help to assemble the pieces. It's not a bad idea to study the cause of failure more closely in any case, so that can be your reason for the change in process."

The work moved forward again with each team leader warned to be on the look-out for problems. They switched to working in pairs which changed around daily. The reason Cal gave was that she wanted to get everyone familiar with all aspects of the project they worked on, but it made it harder for any one person to damage anything.

***

The explosion shook Cal's office and she was out the door and heading to the main level before her mug hit the floor. Landers and Digney were organizing the response to the disaster. Men bleeding and groaning on the floor were being checked by their uninjured team members. A couple of the engineers were tying bandages and giving orders. They worked calmly and efficiently as if the Shed weren't filled with acrid smoke and their ears still ringing from the blast. Cal's heart swelled with pride. She stayed out of their way, checking outside instead.

"Hanson's run for the academy, they have a hospital there to train medics." The guard pointed. "They're comin' now, Commander."

The medics jumped off the coach and ran in the door with their bags and took over. Cal followed at a slower pace. Injured were carried away on stretchers, four men were covered with blankets. Soon only the uninjured were left.

"What happened?" Cal looked at the pieces of the machine shop scattered across the floor.

"Looks like the forge." Landers rubbed his eyes. "The boys were firing it up to get working on Patrick's fan-engine. Few minutes after they loaded the coal and started the bellow, it blew. We were going to forge each blade, grind it to size, then weld them to the central shaft. So I had them set up to be able to pass each piece along to the next stage. Figured it would still take a week to get it assembled. That's why there were so many casualties."

"Don't know anything that could blow a forge up like that, not accidentally anyway." Digney picked up something from the floor. "This doesn't look like a piece of the forge. More like one of the boilers—if we made it real thin."

"Could a boiler blowing cause this much damage?" Cal waved at the equipment knocked over and strewn about. Now that she looked for it, she could see the chaos fanned out from the forge.

"Might, but they'd have noticed a boiler stuck in there." Digney handed her the fragment. "And this is too thin. Wouldn't hold much pressure."

"What if the ball was packed with gunpowder?" Cal peered at the thing in her hand. The inside looked black. She rubbed it with her thumb and it came away smudged. "Bury it under the coal. Then when the forge is heated, the ball fails, the powder explodes and ..." she waved at the mess.

"We'll post guards inside and out of the building." O'Brien came over from where he'd been studying what was left of the forge. "Nobody gets in or out without being checked. Won't stop them if they're determined, but it will slow them down."

"Do that, then focus on the backgrounds of the men working here. Do it over until you find something. Start with anyone who wasn't in the room when the forge blew." Cal waved Tallinan over from where he stood at the bottom of the stairs. "I will need the names of the dead, and their families. I will personally inform them of the incident."

"Commander..." Tallinan started to object, then dropped his eyes. "Aye, Commander."

"I am their commanding officer. It is my responsibility."

*****

Cal stood in the barn outside her home. The stonework had been scrubbed, the floor relaid with fresh planks.

"Let's give it a try." Cal waved at Hans who pulled a long lever. Slowly, then with increasing speed, the roof gaped open. The two halves settled with a thump. "Now closed." Hans moved another lever. A pump began chugging below them. The roof lifted slowly, creaking as the pistons moved at slightly different speeds. The peak closed. Hans let the pump run a moment longer before returning the first lever to its original position to lock the system. Then he turned off the pump.

"I'd say that counts as a success." Cal walked around the barn. "I have a project in mind. I'll need a bolt or two of silk. See if you can pick up fabric that's spoiled or something. As long as it isn't rotten. Wood too, thin enough to be a bit flexible, but not weak. And some rope too.

"I will get it all assembled." Hans looked thoughtful. "You building a kite?"

"Something like that." Cal grinned. "Let's keep the work we do here quiet. With security issues at Shed, we don't need to attract the wrong kind of attention here."

As the work at the Shed restarted, the men looked at each other suspiciously. They were all smart enough to know the explosion was no accident. New people were vetted carefully. As a further precaution, Cal created more separation between the teams, setting up a second workshop for the engine team specific to their needs.

The envelope team had moved from measuring to testing prototypes of possible shapes.

"We have to decide how to create the envelope." Ensign Cesare sat at Cal's table in her office and pointed to drawings he'd laid out. "One possibility is to have a single bag hold the hydrogen. It would be lightest, but perhaps the least stable and most vulnerable to damage. The other possibility would be to make a frame, then stretch the envelope around it. It would make it easy to attach the gondola to the envelope. Dividing the envelope into sections would help because if the envelope were damaged, we wouldn't lose all our lift at once. The Ferandican's airship looks to be a blend of the two. They don't have a complete frame, but the envelope is reinforced at top and bottom. It saves weight and yet gives a bit more stability. We will need to have flaps, like so." He drew quickly on the paper. "To keep the airship from rolling. Think of them as keels, but on four sides. As with a ship, we'll need rudders—one for side to side and one for up and down."

"Let's make a small version of each. We can fly them inside the hall, and test the strengths of each design."

"Aye Commander."

# Chapter 8  - Failure is necessary

The original three teams expanded as Cal added a group to design the gondola, another to work on steering and stabilizing mechanisms.

Models of airships crashed in an amazing variety of ways in the Shed.  Some lost pressure suddenly, while others hit the ceiling or walls and ruptured the envelope. One got too near a lamp and burst into flame. The envelope and steering teams argued through the days about how to make the craft safer.

Amidst all of this, Patrick called Cal to watch the first test of a prototype engine. It spun up as he fed steam into it until it howled painfully loud. Cal yelled at him to shut it down, but the howl became a scream as it tore itself to pieces. Patrick and Cal came out from where they'd taken shelter to find bits of steel were embedded in the wall, ceiling and floor in a ring around the engine.

"It isn't balanced right." Patrick kicked the table. "As soon as it got up to speed the wobble became destructive."

"Learn from it and improve." Cal went back to her office.

Patrick tried putting the engine under load to slow it down, but then the shaft took on the wobble and snapped or flung the props into the walls. Cal had planking installed after a piece of propeller came through the wall and embedded itself in the door across the hall.

Long story short, the engines were incredibly powerful and efficient—until they blew apart.

On the other hand, the boiler team was making progress. They'd surpassed 1500 pounds per square inch of pressure. Landers designed a heavy double valve to manage the extreme strain of the forces involved. Patrick's engines were blowing at 300 psi. Cal was tempted to say the boiler was done, but Landers wanted even higher pressures.

"We can release a tiny stream and reduce its speed to something the engine can handle by increasing the size of the pipe. I want to see how far we can push this."

"Okay, but take extra precautions. These things are creating enough force to do severe damage to the Shed. Build a steel tank big enough to run the test in with large vent tubes to the outside. It will contain the shrapnel and the steam."

O'Brien's security men were everywhere underfoot, and no more major incidents occurred. However, countless minor setbacks set everyone's patience to the test. Fabric for an envelope would be slashed, metal would have impurities which made it weak, pipes sprung leaks. As irritating as all of that was, it didn't slow work nearly as much as the guards' attempts to prevent them from happening.

"This isn't working." Cal looked across her desk at O'Brien who sat stiff and still in one of her chairs. "One of your guys almost took a severe burn because he moved in the wrong direction at the wrong time. So, what we are going to do is move all the security outside the Shed. Lock down everyone who comes in or out during the day. At night, set men inside at each station, but warn them not to touch anything for any reason."

O'Brien nodded once and left.

Cal leaned back in her chair and contemplated the order in front of her. The Lord Admiral Shaunsey was throwing a summer ball. All the members of the Admiralty were expected to attend. Cal had tried to argue she wasn't a proper member, but HRH Hubert told her she was going, and that was that. She would have worn her uniform to match the others around the table, but no one had bothered to create a dress uniform for the Engineers. Cal could take apart and repair engines with ease, but she knew nothing about uniforms.

Time to talk to the expert.

Cal wrote a letter and had Tallinan mail it off immediately, then put it out of her mind. She had a couple of weeks yet before she had to deal with this nonsense.

***

While the work at the Shed progressed, Cal kept spending a few mornings a week on the wall. Gradually her arms stopped turning into limp rope after a few minutes climbing. This morning she had set a goal of getting past a tricky spot with a long reach. Nothing she'd tried had got her past it. Her fingers missed the hold by inches. She couldn't reach it normally. Her arms weren't long enough. The spot haunted her dreams.

This morning Cal decided to try something new. Instead of staying spread out on the wall, she

126

gripped the last handhold with white fingers and brought her feet up to holds not far below her hands. Instead of looking like a spider on the wall, she positioned herself like a frog.

Bouncing a little, then more, until she didn't think she could hold on anymore, Cal pushed hard with her legs and as her weight passed her hands she threw them up ahead of her. They caught hold of the next hold. One on the right looked close. Cal climbed up past the gap, concentrating on making the next move.

One more reach forced her to bounce her weight up, but she'd started using her legs for more push. A few more feet and her next hold was a bar at the top of the wall. Another bar further in and Cal hoisted herself to the platform at the top.

"Congratulations, Commander. Ring the bell to let everyone know you made it." A wiry sailor grinned at her.

After clanging her victory, Cal looked around at the Academy. The Shed showed just above a copse of trees which lined this side of the path. The Academy building looked different from up here. She was astonished to see cannons mounted on the roof.

"Fortunately, going down is easy. First, you need leg loops like a bosun's' chair." He showed her again how to tie it, then had her double-check her work before he checked again. "If you are doing a straight rappel, you'll only have the one harness, so you want it perfect because you're trusting your life to it. Some people will wear an extra belt to give another place to clip the rope." He attached the big clip the loop he'd had her make and the safety harness, too. She double-checked the rope's attachment to the ring, then he told her to toss the rope down the wall. He handed her a pair of gloves which fit snugly on her hands.

"Stand at the edge, holding the rope in your right hand. Lean back, keep your back straight. Now gradually let the rope slide until you are standing on the face of the wall with your back to the ground. Walk down the wall as you let the rope slide through your hand."

The trip to the bottom was much quicker than going up. Cal grinned as she pushed off and dropped the last couple of feet to the ground.

"We'll make a climber of you for sure." Clarke helped her untie the ropes and get out of the harness.

Cal tilted her head back and looked up the wall.

"Beat you."

As a reward for her victory, Twost led her in a wild gallop back to the Shed.

***

Back in the barn outside her home, Cal allowed herself to relax and experiment with all the things she held back from at the Shed. A steel ball three feet across sat in one corner. It was one that rated up to the 1500 psi. Landers didn't failure test it because he knew the design wouldn't go any higher. Cal rescued it off the scrap heap with Bundo's help and brought to the barn. What she discovered was once the pressure was up on the ball, it never dropped below 1000 psi even without a fire to heat it. She used a copy of Lander's valve to control the flow so she didn't have to light the fire much.

She couldn't take one of Patrick's engines as they all failed spectacularly. The kid was determined and each test lasted a minute or so longer than the last. He'd given up on trying for precise balance and was working on a vibration dampening system. Cal had convinced a blacksmith to make a ridiculous number of what he called steel teeth. She welded the teeth onto the shaft, then painstakingly balanced it. By placing either end on a support and waiting for it to settle into a resting position, she was able to pinpoint the heavier teeth and file them down. After three tedious weeks of work, the shaft and blades no longer rotated on their own. Now, she fitted the conical shell around it. It all attached to a four-bladed prop which the engine team had made then discarded because it was too big.

Hans laughed at her for getting a leather blouse made, but it kept sparks from lighting her clothes on fire. The welder's goggles completed the outfit. Fortunately, Hans was no artist so Cal was safe from finding a picture of her in her work gear pinned to her door. Not to mention after the first time he'd lit his pants on fire, he'd seen the wisdom of her outfit.

She'd rescued a pile of silk fabric thrown out because of the tear. By cutting pieces out around it, she'd made an envelope which filled most of the barn and as far as she could tell, held pressure. To be on the safe side, she'd double-layered the envelope fabric, staggering the seams. After she sewed them, she then glued them as well.

What took up space in the barn now was a single beam with the high-pressure tank, engine and prop mounted on it. She'd got Hans to help her build a floor, then made a frame from wooden slats to glue fabric to for a tent to shelter her from the cold and wind.

In her design, control for the speed would come from a single lever. Instead of stabilizers and rudders, Cal made a single vertical fin at the rear of the envelope. Then large fins on either side of the gondola which she could tilt independently of each other.

The inspiration for the fins came from the project she had finished, but not found enough nerve to test. Hans called it the Kite, and with a strong enough wind, she and the students had actually been able to fly it on a rope, very much like a kite. Cal didn't intend for it to be attached to a rope for use. The last time she'd tried it, she'd had them fly it with her hanging on to a crossbar with her hips and legs on slings. She'd never been so terrified in her life. The Kite had shaken and tumbled, almost throwing her off.

Seeing it standing in the corner made her feel guilty, so on one of her raiding trips to the Shed, she and Bundo had carried it up the roof and put it in the small barn on the top where she didn't have to look at it.

Tonight, Cal inspected all the pieces of the ship but didn't adjust anything. She'd gotten a reply from Crysabel saying that she and Pentam were coming to town and would visit Cal soon.

"What does the Admiralty think of your hobby?" Hans slipped in the door.

"They don't know. I plan to keep it that way." Cal looked up from the seam she was inspecting. "Pentam and Crysabel here?"

"They have just arrived. I've put them in the parlour to wait for you."

"I'll hurry or some student will get Pentam talking and they'll be up all night."

"I believe it may be too late." Hans grinned at her. "He had me carry an extraordinarily heavy box up to your studio. Very pleased with himself, too".

"I will refrain from exploring it until after supper."

Cal ran to the back door and up the servants' stairs to her room. Donning one of her simpler gowns, she ran her fingers through her hair and checked for visible smudges.

"Crysabel, you're simply glowing." Cal ran into the parlour to take her friend's hands. "I'm glad to see you well."

"Mother decided a trip to the city to shop for her favourite ship's Captain wasn't going to wear me out too badly. Pentam needed to come in to arrange something for his thesis presentation too, so here we are, ready to help you dress to kill."

"Do you have a date set?" Cal looked over at Pentam, who twirled a glass of wine in his fingers.

"Tentatively, for October, after the baby is born. Crysabel is going to bring him to the presentation to get an early start on his education."

"Oh, you." Crysabel tossed a bun at him which Pentam neatly caught and devoured. "And what if the babe's girl?"

"She can still come, but I'll need a second job to properly keep you and her in dresses."

Beth knocked on the door to announce supper, so they trooped into the dining room to devour her good cooking.

After supper, Cal retreated with Pentam and Crysabel to her studio, the only room aside from her bedroom where they could have privacy.

"What's this mysterious box Hans told me about?"

"It's a gift for your friend in high places." Pentam crouched to unlatch the lid and lift it away.

"The strange drawing!"

"Yes, it was a great puzzle." Pentam ran his finger along the tightly coiled copper wire which made a C shape on either side of a piece of black metal. "You recall I mentioned batteries. I made one to play around with. Copper carries the current best of what I've found. When I was trying to make the coil at first I wrapped it around a nail. One time I forgot to unhook the battery from the wire. Imagine my shock when the nail acted like a magnet, but only when the wires were attached to the battery. That suggested the piece in the middle was a magnet. It took some doing to find one this big. The coils were easy from there. I've wound them on wood to hold them. Watch this." He attached a copper wire to each post of the battery, and the magnet began spinning.

"An engine?" Cal reached out but didn't touch the thing.

"It will carry a load depending on the size of the battery." Pentam unhooked the battery, then held the wires in one hand without quite allowing them to touch. He fastened a handle to the magnetic spindle and cranked. Sparks jumped between the wires. "I'm not sure what use it is other than a curiosity at this time, but I'm sure some bright engineer will come up with something." Pentam winked at Cal.

"This is amazing." Cal leaned closer to look. "I can see it used for small winches where a steam engine doesn't make sense. It depends on how long the battery will last, of course. If you were near a steam engine a couple of cogs would keep the generator going without a battery."

"What did I tell you?" Pentam grinned at his wife. "I can work with theory and ideas, but Cal's the one to put them to use."

***

In the morning Cal sent a message to the Admiralty asking for a meeting and for the Crown Prince to attend if possible. Then she and Crysabel hired a coach and went looking for a dress.

They finally settled on one with a cream-coloured skirt and sleeves. A black satin vest laced over top with front, back and each side tapering to a point which rested on the skirt. With the embroidered version of her Royal Engineer sigil sewn on the breast, it would look enough like a uniform to shock the stuffier members of society. When Cal compared it to her leather vest and goggles in the barn she had a fit of giggles.

The seamstress said she'd have the dress ready in a week for the fitting, so Cal and Crysabel paused for tea in a shop before heading home. Much to their surprise, a coach waited outside the house with the royal crest on it.

Pentam met Cal at the door.

"No, His Highness isn't waiting in the parlour, but he sent his coach to fetch you immediately upon your arrival at home. For some reason, he thinks you asking for a meeting is some kind of emergency."

"I have to admit; I spend more energy trying to get out of the meetings than I put into them. I must have piqued his curiosity." Cal shrugged. "No matter, let's grab your box and go show them your genius."

"Me?" Pentam's voice squeaked. "I don't want to explain that thing in front of the Crown Prince and the Admiralty."

"Who better?" Cal pointed upstairs. "Go pack it up and I'll send Hans to help you carry it down."

Pentam quivered all the way to the Academy. At least there, Cal could grab two burly guards to carry the box.

"You have gold in this thing, Commander?" one asked.

"Better." Cal pushed open the door and directed them to set it on the table.

HRH Hubert lounged in his seat, but three of the Admirals including Vice-Admiral Peysk sat bolt upright to get a better look.

"So Commander, what's this about?" The Crown Prince leaned forward. "If this isn't worth my time, I'll promote you to Admiral and make you sit through each and every meeting in its entirety."

"Your Highness, may I present Pentam Booksdale?"

"Yes, I remember sea serpents and I crashed your wedding." The prince nodded at Pentam.

"Your intelligence service's attempts to steal an invention from the Zithayan Dynasty caused me considerable trouble." Cal frowned at him. "I'm still annoyed we were used as a cover."

"You can hardly expect us to announce we're sending out spies."

"True, but if other countries start connecting science expeditions with spies, it won't be long before our expeditions aren't welcome." Cal took a deep breath. "But that's a discussion for another day. I have a confession to make, then I will turn things over to Pentam. While in the Dynasty, I happened across a very rough sketch of some kind of machine. I took it from a man who'd probably got it from the dead man at the end an alley in Zithaya, so it's reasonable. It was after that incident the officials decided to do customs inspections on all the ships looking for illicit art, which being paper would allow them to search for plans for a machine they wanted kept secret. I had to burn the original, then when we were at sea, tried to recreate it. I gave that sketchbook to Mr. Booksdale here as the person I trusted the most to make sense of the diagram." Cal bowed to the prince. "If you decide to punish me for my actions, I won't argue, but please wait until Pentam has finished his explanation."

The Crown Prince frowned at her but nodded once.

Pentam stepped forward, unlatched the box and lifted the lid off.

"If you are interested, I can go over the stages by which I arrived at this contraption." He attached the wires to the battery and the magnet began to spin. "What we have here is an engine which runs on electricity. That is the movement of charge from one place to another. The greater the charge, the greater the power. With a sufficiently large source of power, this could be useful for winches and other small tasks where steam engines would be too cumbersome." He took the wires off the battery. "If you are wondering where we would find such a source." Pentam attached the crank and began spinning the magnet. Sparks leapt between the wires in his hand.

"I think I may just forgive you, Commander Shillingsworth." The prince stood up to look more closely at the machine. "How difficult is this to make?"

"Once you know the principles involved, it is very simple." Pentam motioned at the engine. "It is a magnet spinning between coils of copper wire. I could think of ways to make it more efficient, but it is not a complicated machine."

"Gentlemen, I don't see a strategic value in keeping this engine a secret. Releasing it might take pressure off our other project which is of extreme importance." The Prince gave Cal a long look. "I had hoped to hear a report that we had a functioning airship."

"We are very close. We are, in fact, closer than the official reports suggest." Cal steadied herself on the table. "Commanding the Royal Engineers is not nearly as satisfying as getting dirty and playing with ideas, but we need the breadth of experience and vision they bring to the project."

"Why do I get the feeling you are going to say 'but' just about here?"

"I've been working on my own ideas in a space I control. The project goal is a large impressive airship. I'm building something which will hold one or two people and prove our designs will work. As you know, we have been plagued with petty sabotage. Where there is sabotage, there is no reason why there couldn't also be the theft of designs. I expect as we succeed with each step, someone will try to steal the plans, either to sell them or give them to another country."

"So, you're saying we're doing the work for other countries? What about security?" The Vice-Admiral almost banged the table but stopped his fist just above the surface.

"We have dozens of people working on the project, plus as many trying to guard it. Locking everything down tight only made our work more dangerous. So I've been taking another tack."

"Indeed." The Prince leaned back and peered at her.

"All the work from each team is brought to me. They have operational plans which are changed and marked up on a daily basis. I take those plans and make a clean copy for our records, which I get Petty Officer Tallinan to file in the locked room to which only the Chief Petty Officer and I have keys for. Any attempt to steal the plans will focus on that room. So, I leave one or two essential details out of the plans or change something. I keep a record of what those changes are in a secure location in my office which only I know about. If someone were to steal the designs without making the corrections, the results would range from failure to catastrophic."

The prince started laughing.

"I knew there was a reason I liked you. Keep us appraised of your progress, official and unofficial. Intelligence will be instructed to pay close attention to what is going on around your Shed. Maybe we can catch a spy or two." He pointed at Pentam. "Be ready to announce your invention at the Royal Science Society in, shall we say a week? You and Cal can cook up something dramatic to catch the people's attention."

"Yes, Your Highness." Pentam bowed, while Cal nodded. Inwardly, though, she was rolling her eyes. Between balls and this presentation, she wasn't getting much work done in the coming week.

# Chapter 9  - New Connections

Pentam's presentation of what he'd taken to calling the electric engine was a huge hit. When he offered free instructions for anyone to make their own, playing with electricity became an obsession with people through the city.

One evening a few days after his talk, a visitor appeared at the door of Cal's home.

"This one heard the inventor of the lightning engine is staying here." The speaker's clothes reminded Cal of the people of the Zithayan Dynasty. An oddly shaped coach had parked in the yard.

"He is indeed here, come in." Cal stepped back. The woman bowed and entered the home. Pentam was in the parlour, debating with the students as he enjoyed doing in the evenings.

"They keep me sharp and humble," he'd said. Crysabel sat in the corner, a small smile playing across her face as she watched.

"Pardon the rambunctious atmosphere." Cal led the visitor to the parlour. "My pardon, may I have your name to introduce you?"

"Hyansea Kee Dolichak. You would call me the assistant to the ambassador."

"We are honoured by your presence." Cal pushed the door open, and the babble paused.

"A woman from the Zithayan Embassy has come to visit us, Hyansea Kee Dolichak."

The woman bowed low and took a seat graciously offered by one of the students.

"This one is asked to speak to the inventor of the lightning engine."

"I developed this version," Pentam said. "What may I do for you?"

"We were working on such a thing, but it didn't work as well as what you showed."

"You were there?"

"This one was sent to answer the invitation to our embassy."

"I am honoured." Pentam bowed in his seat.

"You gave away the plans on how to build this thing. Why?"

"I didn't feel right making money from it. Giving the instructions away also means hundreds, maybe thousands of people are trying to improve it and learn how it may be used." Cal could see Pentam fighting the guilt of being hailed as the inventor of the machine. Taking credit for another's work was as bad as murder in his eyes.

"The ambassador sent a copy of your plans and instructions to the Chief Bureaucrat. Your Prince said it was to be shared with everyone."

"That's right. If you have any questions I would happy to discuss them with you."

"The ambassador expects an invitation will come for you to speak at the Bureaucratic University. This one would be honoured if you accept."

"I would be happy to—"

Crysabel cleared her throat. Pentam looked over at her and turned red. They gazed into each other's eyes until Crysabel nodded and Pentam heaved a sigh.

"We would be happy to accept your invitation, after the birth of our child and they are able to travel. I also have an obligation to fill during that period. However, if you are willing to wait until November...?"

"This one is honoured to carry your words to the ambassador." She stood up and bowed.

"Please stay and take some refreshment." Cal stepped over to her.

It was as if a ripple ran through the woman. When it had gone, she stood differently and had a smile on her face.

"Please call me Hyansea. I would be delighted to enjoy your hospitality. I heard of something called scones, Commander Shillingsworth."

"Please call me Cal here. I will ask Beth to bring scones and jam. What would you like to drink?"

"I have to admit to a fondness for your red wine."

"Pentam, perhaps you will get Hyansea a glass?"

Cal slipped out to check with Beth in the kitchen. She helped load a tray with a pile of scones and dishes of jam, then carried it to the parlour, just in time to hear Hyansea finish what sounded like an explanation.

"...when I speak for the Bureaucracy, I must use the formal language. It doesn't translate well into your Anglian. When I speak for myself I may use the familiar."

"I have read about it Hyansea, but never heard for myself." One of the students sat beside the visitor. "It was in Barlowe's translation of The Soul of Governance."

"Barlowe did a well enough job, but he, of course, missed much of the nuance of the discourse." Hyansea sipped from her wine glass.

"Understood, he was working not only with a different language, but the metered lines. Is it true the meaning of a word changes depending on where it lands in rhythm?"

"Very much so. The word which Barlowe translates as 'duty' really should be read as 'obligation' if it is a light step, and you don't have an easy word to say what we mean for the heavy step. It comes closest if you read it as the action you will die to accomplish."

Cal put the tray down on the table and smiled at Hyansea. The woman bowed her head briefly then picked up a scone to take a bite out of it. She closed her eyes.

"I can see why the Under-Secretary of Customs was so adamant we try these. We have nothing like them at home." She finished the scone, and the student beside her pointed to the untouched jam dish.

"You really must try them with the blackberry jam." He cut a scone open and spread jam on it for Hyansea.

When the tray was empty Hyansea stood up again.

"I really must return."

"I hope I haven't made trouble for you," Cal said as she guided Hyansea to the door.

"Not at all. We are not ordered but encouraged to interact with the people and culture around us. You'd be surprised at how a small detail of culture can create or destroy understanding between people."

"In that case, you are most welcome to visit at any time. Feel free to bring someone along if they wish."

"And I was told the Anglians had little subtlety." Hyansea smiled. "I will extend your welcome."

*** 

Crysabel fussed with the finishing touches on the gown Cal was wearing to the Lord Admiral's Summer Ball.

"It is too bad you keep your hair so short; there isn't much I can do with it."

"That's entirely the point." Cal grinned. "I don't have the time to fuss."

"It suits you." Crysabel poked through the jewellery box on Cal's dresser. "You must have something to add.

"I'm not much for jewelry," Cal shrugged. "Most of those were my mother's and I can't bear to get rid of them."

"What about this?" Crysabel held up a tiny lens set in brass hanging from a chain.

"Pentam gave that to me." Cal took the chain and looked more closely at the lens. "I used it to see tiny details for my sketches; when I came ashore I must have put it in the box."

Crysabel slipped the chain over Cal's head. It gleamed on the black satin bodice.

"Perfect." She gave Cal a push. "Your coach will be here. Go on. Pentam and I will arrive fashionably late and probably leave unfashionably early. But I have to see you turning heads in this gown."

Cal rode alone in the coach to the Lord Admiral's city home. She stepped out at the bottom of a long flight of steps, a lantern placed on each one. By the time she'd reached the top, she was thinking of ways to make stairs easier. A servant escorted her to the entry of the ballroom where she was announced. As she had planned, there weren't many people there yet and none paid her any attention, but thankfully, neither did they snub her. She found a corner and watched as more guests arrived. The room filled with people and conversation. A few people came over to talk to Cal, most to ask how she was managing since her father's death.

Hyansea entered on the arm of an older man announced as the Ambassador. From the way they moved, Cal guessed they were in formal mode for the night. Her stomach growled, so she wandered past the buffet table and picked up a little to calm her stomach, and a glass of wine to calm her nerves.

The ambassador of the Kershian Empire was announced and Cal glanced over, then almost choked on her wine.

Bri Curzem wore a jet-black uniform. It looked both formal and utilitarian. She could imagine him wearing it while going through the minutia of his day. Cal headed over to talk to him. Bri turned to face her after greeting the Admiral of Coastal Defense. His eyes widened in recognition, then he smiled.

"I should have known they wouldn't keep you hidden away on your ship for long." He bowed over her hand, then somehow she found herself walking beside him with her fingers on his arm. "I am glad indeed to see you well."

"Ambassador, now." Cal let him lead her to the buffet table for another glass of wine. "Congratulations. If I'd known, I might have come to visit."

"Sadly, the Emperor doesn't encourage his Ambassadors to fraternize with the people around us, particularly the Anglians. I am glad the Emperor isn't here, so whatever chastisement he sends for enjoying myself will be months in coming."

"It is too bad. Friends are easier to live with than strangers."

"Or enemies." Bri helped himself to a plate of food. Cal followed suit, then sat with him at a table.

"You may wish to find another companion. It will not do your career any good to be seen being too friendly with the Kershian Ambassador. War is on the horizon, as much as sensible people detest it. The world, however, is not run by sensible people."

"Until I am ordered otherwise, I will be friends with whomever I choose," Cal announced coolly.

"A noble and foolish sentiment." Bri toasted her with a glass of wine a servant had placed at his elbow. "I wish there were many more of you. Too many are like the man staring at you as if he would like nothing better than to stab you repeatedly with a knife."

Cal looked over without moving her head and sighed. "Lord Sifton. We are not each other's favourite people." She sipped at her wine. "Tell me, did you learn anything about the lightning machine? It is mere curiosity, so don't feel you need to answer if it is not a topic you're comfortable with."

"We barely got a sniff. Imagine the shock at my Embassy when we were invited to the introduction of a new engine and saw your Mr. Booksdale working the thing as if it were the latest fashion. We now have a full set of plans and instructions. I suspect they are being examined to determine where the trap is laid. Alas, I fear it will be months before any official recognition of the thing happens. Some tourist will bring home plans and build one before our esteemed scientists."

Cal chuckled. "I wonder if part of the impetus for the gift to the world thinking was a test of relations with other countries. People who plan betrayal will see plots everywhere."

"Too true." He lifted his glass with a wry smile.

The orchestra tuned up and began to play, and Bri sighed.

"As much as I would enjoy a dance with you, my Lady, I fear even you would find the consequences unfortunate. I will make my farewells and leave you to your countrymen."

He stood, bowed over her hand, then walked through the room, chatting with a person here and there before making his exit.

Lord Sifton had a cluster of people around him and was talking earnestly. He glanced in her direction often enough Cal concluded she was the subject of their conversation. Cal thought about another glass of wine but settled on water.  She meandered through the room, talking to those she recognized and being introduced to more people than she could remember.

As promised Pentam and Crysabel made an appearance, made a circuit of the room so the ladies could coo over the coming child. They left soon after.

"His Highness Prince Alfred," intoned a deep voice from the entryway as a younger version of the Crown Prince sauntered into the room. Cal watched him curiously. He was the first royalty she'd seen other than Prince Hubert. Prince Alfred stopped in front of her.

"You have to be Lady Shillingsworth." He inclined his head slightly as Cal curtseyed. "My brother has said you are a brilliant engineer. I am glad to have you working for us, though I must confess to utter ignorance about engines and such."

"What does interest you, Your Highness?"

He tilted his head at her and eyed her for a long couple of breaths.

"The arts, Lady Shillingsworth. What worth is it to have a secure and powerful nation, if we don't have the desire to create and celebrate beauty?"

"Indeed, Your Highness, art is the pulse of a nation."

"The pulse of a nation." Prince Alfred nodded his head. "I may just quote you when I beg for more funding for the frivolous." His voice twisted on the last word.

"I would be honoured." Cal curtseyed again.

"If you'll forgive me, Lady Shillingsworth, I must speak to more people. A gallery to hold the best of our nation's creative work is a dream of mine. I need to convince those who hold the purse strings of Anglia to loosen them in the name of art."

"If I may be so bold, your Highness, you may tell those you speak with that Lady Shillingsworth is an enthusiastic supporter of your dream."

"How enthusiastic?" Prince Alfred raised his eyebrows. His eyes looked doubtful. Clearly, others were happy to declare delight and less happy to act.

"I believe 20,000 sovereigns worth of enthusiasm. My business manager will have a draft ready for you when you require it."

"You're not joking, are you?" Prince Alfred briefly raised his hand to his temple as though he suddenly felt lightheaded. When he took and kissed her hand, she thought his eyes had an extra glisten to them. "Lady Shillingsworth, I am touched beyond your knowing."

"What on Earth did Prince Alfred find to talk to you about?" The Vice-Admiral asked once the young prince was a safe distance away.

"Art."

"Ah, yes, he's the sensitive one of the family."

Cal bristled at his dismissive tone.

"Vice-Admiral, when you teach young men to defend their country with their lives, do you ever talk about what they are defending?"

"What are you talking about?"

"The Navy exists to protect Anglia, so we can have people like Prince Alfred who desire to make the world a more beautiful place."

"I haven't heard it put that way before, but I can't argue with you. If we were all warriors, life would be dull indeed."

Cal headed home soon after. She spent the coach ride planning how she would explain the huge gift to her business manager. It would make no difference to how she lived, though it would mean they might have fingers in fewer pies. Smiling, she pulled her coat closer. It would be worth it to see the prince's dream come to fruition.

# Chapter 10 - Disastrous Demonstration

The week after the ball, a messenger delivered a missive to Cal's office. The Crown Prince had been invited to view the demonstration of a radically different kind of steam engine and he wanted her to be present. Cal's stomach went cold and she had to stop herself from checking on the plans in the room, or her record of the mistakes she'd place in them.

She wasn't the only person working on steam engines. She knew of two shops which were involved in a race to produce a better way to use steam to drive machines. The address on the invitation wasn't either of those shops, though.

The coach the Prince had sent to fetch her would be arriving soon. Cal had been working on

Patrick's newest incarnation of the fan engine. Her clothes were covered with grease and metal dust and she had no time to change.

The driver of the coach didn't even raise an eyebrow at her appearance. He opened the door for her, then climbed up and set out almost before she'd taken her seat. The coach had something which smoothed out the ride. She'd have to make an excuse to crawl under it one day and investigate. They pulled up in front of a new brick building. One of the prince's guards met her at the door.

"His Highness is waiting for you, Commander."

"Lead on."

The guard walked her into a long room where a medium-sized boiler already radiated heat. The pressure looked to be over 400 psi. A respectable level, she admitted to herself. The pipe out of the boiler ran straight to a conical steel casing. A pipe came out the other end pointing up at the ceiling, probably to safely vent the steam. A shaft ended with something which looked like an oversized ship's screw. People were gathered around it, while the prince stood in a bubble of space created by his bodyguards.

"Cal," the Prince called, "come over and give me your opinion."

She wound through the crowd and peered more closely at the setup.

"The shield looks all right. Not quite the angle I think would be most efficient, but for a prototype, it isn't bad."

A man wearing a leather apron over a suit frowned at her. He opened his mouth, but another man wearing a suit but no apron put a hand on his arm to forestall him.

Cal turned the screw by hand. The slightest grinding buzzed under her fingers. When she turned it not quite a half spin, it slowly rotated back the original position. She tried again the other way and got the same result.

"It will be very dangerous to run a test in a room full of people." Cal pointed to the screw. "The shaft is out of balance; something is rubbing inside the casing. It might be all right if the test is kept at low pressure, but even then, I'd be concerned. We've found the failure point very hard to predict."

"The design is sound, it is safe." The man in the apron stepped forward quickly, almost as if he planned to strike Cal. One of the bodyguards put out an arm.

"How many times have you tested the design to the failure point?" Cal waved at the room. "I don't see any damage, so either you haven't done the test, or you have a different shop."

"Your Highness, please don't let Lady Shillingsworth's professional jealousy affect your opinion. She is not the only person capable of thinking creatively." He glared in her direction in contradiction to his obsequious manner.

"He's right, of course," Cal said. "And I would be delighted to see a successful test. I don't care who gets the glory for the design. My concern is the lack of some basic safety precautions."

More people were crowding into the room as she spoke and dread clutched at her. She didn't want to say it in public, but she recognized the design as an early version of the fan engine which shook itself apart even at relatively low pressures. At 400 psi, it would be a bomb.

"I personally guarantee your safety, Your Highness." The man without the apron spoke up.

How? Cal shifted uneasily.

HRH Hubert looked at his bodyguards and lifted an eyebrow. They sighed and he nodded.

"Proceed."

The crowd had filled up the space around them. If it came apart it would impossible for anyone to escape without injury. Taking a deep breath, Cal planted herself between the Prince and the engine.

"Commander, what are you doing?" From his tone, the Crown Prince was annoyed.

"I have a duty to protect you." Cal didn't turn around. She stiffened as bodyguards took her arms. "I've seen what happens if these engines fail. With me between you and the engine, you have a better chance of survival."

"Very well, but we will discuss this later." The hands receded. "If it does go bad what would you recommend?" He whispered in her ear.

"You won't have time to react. I will try to warn you, but this early version is very unstable. You will do best to dive to the floor toward the boiler. The damage will be in a ring around the engine."

"I hope you are wrong."

"So do I, Your Highness."

The men in suits took their positions, the one without the apron at the valve by the boiler. The other positioned himself across the engine from the Prince.

"The steam comes out of the boiler at high pressure and strikes blades inside the casing, setting the shaft to spinning. As the steam expands, the blades grow larger, thus the shape of the case. With this system, we can drive the shaft at speeds not achievable by traditional steam engines. In addition, the high pressure can spin up the shaft very quickly, reaching top speed almost instantly."

The man at the valve cranked it open. As steam roared out of the boiler, the familiar howl of the fan engine filled Cal's ears.

"Cover your ears, Your Highness," she shouted as she covered her own. Under the howl, a whining grew. She heard at least one blade scrape the inside of the casing. The screw jumped from a dead stop to a blur in the blink of an eye. Thumping shook the table, showing the thing was further out of true than she'd thought.

"Shut it down!" Cal yelled over the cacophony. The man with the apron turned to say something to his partner just as the casing failed, sending a jet of blistering steam into his face. He screamed and staggered back. The other man reached for the valve but pulled his hand back with a curse. The thumping grew worse.

"Oh God, help us," Cal whispered. Something slammed into her from behind, throwing her to the floor. Someone was shouting for people to get to the ends of the room. With her hands knocked away from her ears, the roar of the engine sounded demonic, drowning out every other sound—even the pounding of her heart.

The noise of the engine disintegrating was entirely different. It screamed like a mortally wounded animal as it tore itself apart. After what felt like a lifetime, the thumping stopped. The resulting silence seemed...strange.

Cal tried to move, but bodies on top of her pinned her painfully to the brick floor.

"That's the last time I ignore your advice, Cal." The Crown Prince muttered in her ear and she sighed in relief, then gasped at a sharp pain in her side. The weight vanished. She tried to push herself up, but again the pain hit her like a blow. "Get her out of here," the prince ordered sharply. "Take her to my personal physician. Meanwhile, get some help in here. Send in the coachman, the guards, everyone to help with the injured."

Firm hands lifted Cal to carry her out of the room. Even in her pain, she couldn't help noticing the bits of metal protruding from the ceiling and walls. People lay moaning covered with blood, some blistering from the superheated steam.

"Wet sheets for the burns," Cal said and coughed, crying out from the pain. His Highness looked over at her, blood dripped from his scalp as he knelt beside a man whose stump of an arm pumped red over the prince's arms. Then the swiftly-moving bodyguards had taken her from the room. They bundled her gently into the coach, where she let the tears come, refusing to sob.

The wild ride through the streets finally ended before a building that seemed familiar, but her blurry vision kept her from recognizing it. Gentle hands lifted her from the carriage, and then someone was snapping orders as they brought her into a room. It didn't look like an infirmary, more like a parlour. Strange, but she didn't have the energy to really think about it.

"Lay her on the table," a new voice ordered them. A face shaped leaned over her. "Does it pain you to breathe? You're bleeding on the left."

"I am?" Cal whispered.

Firm hands felt her side until she sucked in a breath and bit back a curse.

"I'm told you're a Navy Commander. Go ahead and swear if you must," advised the voice dryly. A hand with a cloth mopped the tears from her eyes. "We are going to sit you up. I'm sorry, I must cut away your clothes to fix your ribs. I can send them out of the room, but I may need them if you faint. A fall from the table could kill you in your condition.

"I don't have the energy for modesty." Cal forced out the words between waves of pain, her eyes closed. Cool air brushed her skin where it shouldn't. The doctor muttered something under his breath. She refused to look down.

"Breathe in as much air as you can. Expand your chest even if it hurts."

Cal sucked in air until she thought she might burst, she felt the doctor's hands on her left side, then with a clunk that made her curse, something moved and the pain lessened.

Soft cloth wrapped around her and for a moment the pain grew worse again, then it settled to a manageable level.

She opened her eyes. The two bodyguards stood at ease their eyes carefully looking over her head. A grey-haired man stood close as he fastened the cloth with a pin.

"Jacket." He put out his hand and one of the guards peeled off his uniform coat to hand to the doctor. The weight and warmth helped Cal relax.

The door to the room burst open. Two men who dwarfed the prince's bodyguards stepped through and took up position on either side of the door. A woman in a plain black dress walked through the door. The bodyguards dropped their knee. The doctor put his hand on Cal's arm.

"Don't move," he admonished in an undertone before bowing deeply. "Your Majesty. This woman is injured, and unable to give obeisance."

"Understood. We are not so proud We must have people injure themselves on Our behalf." She looked at the kneeling guards. "When a squad of the royal guards rides at double time out of the palace grounds, We worry for the safety of our son."

"His Highness is safe and well, Your Majesty. I am told that he remained to coordinate rescue efforts."

"We are relieved." Her Majesty Wilhemeena, Queen of Anglia walked over to examine Cal. "You must be Commander Shillingsworth. Hubert insisted a commission and a new branch of the Navy was essential for your success." She reached out and touched the jacket. "James, ask Cianna to attend with more suitable clothes for the Commander. Something easy to dress in, we don't want to undo Dr. Grant's good work."

"Now, Commander. Report." The Queen met Cal's eyes, her gaze as sharp as a sword.

"Yes, Your Majesty. His Highness requested me to attend a demonstration of a new engine. I was first concerned to see that it looked like an early version of what the Royal Engineers were working on. I also noted several flaws which increased the odds of catastrophic failure. Unfortunately, my assessment was correct." Cal closed her eyes at the memory of the bloodied people scattered through the room.

"Your Majesty, Commander Shillingsworth placed herself between His Highness and the engine when he insisted on seeing the demonstration," the jacketless bodyguard said, looking down at the floor.

"Did you now?" The Queen looked at Cal. "That's normally the job of his guards."

"As an officer in the Royal Navy, His Highness' safety is my concern." Despite her weariness, Cal refused to break eye contact with the queen.

An older woman with a dress over her arm knocked at the door.

"Come in, Cianna." Queen Wilhemeena waved at the bodyguards and Doctor Grant. "Thank you, you may go. Doctor, if you wish, order transport to help Hubert."

The three men bowed and left the room. The Queen's guards stepped out the door and closed it behind them.

"Now Cianna, see what you can do for the Commander."

The woman helped Cal to stand as she pulled the pants away and replaced them with a skirt which wrapped around in a style Cal remembered from when she was a child. A soft tunic covered her torso, then an under-bodice, an overskirt, and finally a satin bodice. She gritted her teeth against the twinges from her ribs.

"Now you are properly modest if out of fashion." A faint smile touched the queen's lips. "Thank you, Cianna. Please have tea sent to us while we await His Highness' return. Ask the guard to direct him to this room."

The woman curtsied and left.

"Please sit, We need not stand on ceremony in private, and We would not keep someone prepared to give her life for our son standing while injured." The Queen sat gracefully in a chair and pointed to another across from her. "The dress suits you; Beatrice had very similar colouring."

Cal ran her hand along the skirt, a lump growing in her throat as she absorbed the queen's meaning.

"I don't know what to say, Your Majesty. I remember my mother wearing black for a week when I was very young. I vaguely recall her saying it was in mourning for the princess."

"I think she would have liked you. She had the same impatience with social conventions." The Queen nodded. "Now tell Us more about what it is that you're doing which has my son so excited."

Cal smiled. Where to begin?

"I am leading a team working on an airship."

"So We understand."  Narrowing her eyes at Cal, not in an unfriendly fashion, she proceeded to interrogate her. "Explain why Ferandica's is not good enough for Us. We could purchase one easily enough."

"True, Your Majesty, but from what I have seen, there are issues with the Ferandican design which my team intends to address. Most of what their ships carry is fuel and water, with only a small space for passengers. I expect it wouldn't handle rough weather well. There is more along the same lines." Cal gestured dismissively. "What we are working on will be entirely different, with space for more crew and passengers, a longer range as well as more stability and maneuverability. I suspect the next conflict will be settled by air power. Anglia will have an Air Navy second to none."

"We see. So how close are you to this marvel of the air?"

"Honestly, we have a way to go to create the ship I have in mind, but we are close to a prototype to test our designs and theories."

"It's refreshing to not have someone promising the moon and the stars by Monday," the queen said, again, that faint smile on her face. A knock at the door signalled the arrival of the tea.

"Alfred tells Us you're a patron of the arts." The Queen tilted her head at Cal after the servants had poured the tea, then left them alone once more.

"I was an artist before I became an engineer. Nothing fancy," she added hastily. "Pencil and charcoal."

"A woman of many talents." The Queen waved at Cal's tea. "Drink up before it gets cold."

They were deep in discussion of Prince Alfred's plans when a knock at the door interrupted them. Prince Hubert walked in and bowed to his mother.

"My apologies for taking so long. I needed to reassure Astrid I was still in one piece."

"You are forgiven. It gave Us time to get to know your delightful Commander. Do sit down, you know I don't like people looming over me."

Hubert sat looking stiff and uncomfortable on the chair.

"We couldn't learn anything from the men who put on the demonstration... they both died." He scowled. "Saves us the trouble of hanging them, I guess. They rented the building only a month back. Intelligence is tracking who did the fabricating, but if they spread out the work, it won't tell us much."

"Their motivation is key." Cal put her teacup down. "If they truly thought they could get the jump on the engine with stolen plans, it may have been mercenary. After all, how much would the Navy pay for engines which worked as those poor fools promised? But I wonder if the people behind them had a darker motive. How many people will trust the fan engine once they hear about the disaster?"

"You think someone wanted that to happen?" The Crown Prince looked shocked.

"Given the shoddy way they ran the demonstration, its spectacular failure was almost a guaranteed result. Their backer probably swore up and down these were the newest and best plans, so they didn't need rigorous testing. Add ambition to greed, and you have a fiasco which very nearly killed the Crown Prince."

"I should have listened to you; a lot of people would be alive now if I had."

"What made you move? One moment the thing was screeching like all the devils of hell, the next, I was lying on the floor with a pile of people on top of me."

"It was you, actually. I heard you mutter something like 'God help us,' and I decided it was time to move. Sorry about your ribs. You would have been all right with just me, but my bodyguards landed on us."

"When I think of the alternative, I will happily put up with injured ribs." Cal gave them a tired grin.

"Take some time off to recover, and that's an order, Commander. Doctor Grant will check you out in a week. If he says you're ready for duty then, you may return."

"Yes, Your Highness." Cal closed her eyes and sighed carefully. "If I may be excused, your Majesty?"

"Of course, Commander. Our thanks for your dedication to duty." The Queen nodded her head. "One of the guards will see you home."

Cal stood and cautiously curtsied, then followed a guard toward a coach and home.

# Chapter 11  - New Suspicions

"Lady Shillingsworth will no longer go anywhere without me," Bundo stood immovable as a rock.

"I can't allow non-Navy personnel into this facility." Chief Petty Officer O'Brien looked just as stubborn as Bundo. "I'm sorry, Commander, my orders come from the Admiralty. Even you can't override them."

"Very well." Cal forced her voice to be as icy as she could. "You explain to the Admiralty why all work at the Shed has stopped." She turned to leave. "Let's go."

"You can't do that!" O'Brien stepped in front of her.

"Did you suddenly get a promotion I didn't hear about?" Cal no longer had to work at the coldness. "Are you the Lord Admiral now? Perhaps you're the new heir to the throne and the news hasn't caught up with me yet." Cal pointed to the Shed. "This is my ship, Petty Officer. Nobody tells me what I can and can't do on my ship. Not you, not the Admiralty, not the Queen herself. If I say work stops, it stops. Now."

The engineers formed up, ready to leave, but the guards held them back.

Cal spun and pointed at a cadet.

"You, fetch the Vice-Admiral, on the double. Tell him we're calling an emergency meeting of the Admiralty, right here, right now. And if you see His Highness, invite him to attend."

The young man paled, but after one look at Cal's face he took off at a flat run.

"You go back to work while we wait." O'Brien pointed to the engineers.

"No." Cal stepped up until she was nose to nose with her security chief. "Are you familiar with what happened to the last Navy officer who mutinied? It may be back before your time. I happened to look it up when the Crown Prince gave me this job. They hung him, then buried him as deep underground as they could dig, so his body wouldn't return to the sea even if the ocean washed away the Academy. Then they marked his record with black ink, and read it out loud at every graduation for the next fifty years. His great-grandchildren finally petitioned the Crown to stop, which is why you wouldn't have heard his name."

O'Brien paled and his hands shook, but he stood his ground. Cal didn't move until the Vice-Admiral came out at a trot.

"I've sent messengers to the others. What is going on?"

"We are having a discussion about who is in command of the Royal Engineers. Apparently, O'Brien has decided he is."

"That's not—" O'Brien put his hands up. Bundo stepped forward, but Cal held out her arm.

"It is exactly what this is about." She didn't look at Vice-Admiral Peysk. "Either the Royal Engineers are truly a separate branch of Her Majesty's Navy, and I am their Commander. Or I have been lied to, and forced to serve under false pretenses."

"Oh dear." The Vice-Admiral sighed. "Would it be too much to ask to get a chair while I wait for the others?"

Cal pointed at one of the guards.

"Chair, fetch." He ran into the Shed, his feet banging on the stairs. His steps sounded slower as he returned.

Peysk settled into the chair with a sigh.

"The others will want chairs too." The guard ran back into the shed. As he brought out the chairs, coaches and steam carriages brought the other Admirals, including the Lord Admiral.

"We have a quorum," he said. "What is this all about?"

"You put me in command of the Royal Engineers, correct?"

"Yes."  He frowned at her as if he was about to warn her that he didn't appreciate being summoned to answer foolish questions.

"Then why is this sailor telling me I don't have command of my own ship?"

"Ship? You aren't on a... " One of the other Admirals turned red as he trailed off.

"This Academy is treated as a Navy ship for the purposes of discipline." Vice-Admiral Peysk rubbed his eyes. "There are other precedents. Commander Shillingsworth is quite correct in stating the Shed is her ship."

"But..." The Lord Admiral began to rise.

"Don't say it, Sir." Cal met his eyes. "Not unless you are willing to accept my resignation on the spot."

"We are far enough along, the project can be completed by one of the other engineers," someone supposed aloud.

"Not bloody likely," Landers shouted from where he stood. "*We're* competent engineers. *She*," he pointed at Cal, "is a genius. Not one of the advances we've made would have happened without her dropping hints to us. Commander Shillingsworth has gone out of her way to make us look good. Not one of us is prepared to take her place."

"That's insubordination," the Lord Admiral yelled. "You'll work how I tell you to work."

"Like hell, we will." Lander put his hands out. "Go ahead lock me up, see how much work you'll get done then." The rest of the engineers held their hands out, too.

The royal coach pulled up. The footman ran to open the door.

"His Highness will talk sense into her," someone muttered loudly enough to be heard by everyone.

The Queen took the footman's hand and stepped out of the coach. Everyone went to their knees. Her Majesty walked over to Cal, with HRH Prince Hubert mere steps behind her.

"Lady Shillingsworth, please rise."

Cal stood and waited for the Queen to ask her to explain herself.

"It has come to Our attention the Admiralty doubts the ability of a woman to fully exercise command over men."  Folding her hands primly, she surveyed the kneeling admirals.  "Which one of you wishes to tell Us that We are not the Admiral Royal of the Navy?"

The Admirals sunk lower and no one spoke.

"Mother," Prince Hubert said.

"You may call Us 'Your Majesty' or the 'Admiral Royal'." The Queen's words might have come out of an arctic blizzard for all the warmth they conveyed. "Commander Shillingsworth, explain yourself."

"Aye, Ma'am." Cal took a deep breath and stilled the trembling in her stomach. "After the recent incident, my personal guard requested I go nowhere without him."

"I've never seen him before," the Lord Admiral dared to point out.

"You wouldn't have." Cal crossed her arms to keep herself from shaking. "He's good at what he does. In case you are wondering about his qualifications, among his own people, Bundo would be the equivalent of an Anglian Duke. He was in command of his country's jungle legion when a situation arose which necessitated his departure." Cal relaxed her arms and bowed to the Queen. "I apologize for what must seem a foolish tantrum, but as the Commander of Royal Engineers, I need to know the people around me will obey orders. I cannot work with people who continually check on whether they should follow my commands. As I asked these worthy gentlemen: am I or am I not the Commander of the Royal Engineers?"

"You are." The Queen nodded her head. "The rest of you may rise." She claimed one of the chairs. "We dislike hidden agendas and mistrust secret orders."

"You as the Admiralty invested Commander Shillingsworth as equivalent to Admiral over the Royal Engineers, confirmed in Our name by HRH Hubert, sitting as acting Admiral Royal. If you had doubts, you should not have given her the commission. In this building," she waved her hand at the Shed, "Commander Shillingsworth's word is law and even I would not contradict her except at great need; any more than I would give orders on any of your ships." She stood up. "Now that We have that settled, We wish to see the work Our Royal Engineers have been doing."

Cal nodded at Bundo and led the way into the Shed.

"Admiral on deck!" Landers bellowed as he and every other engineer stood at attention, holding a salute.

The Queen nodded at them, then spent the next hour listening to explanations of the different aspects of the airship's design. The last place she visited was Cal's office.

"Wait outside," the queen instructed her guards before closing the door behind her and settling into one of the chairs. "We understand your frustration at the foolishness of old men, but know if you do something like this again, Commander, We will grant you command of a ship of the line and send you to patrol the Arctic Ocean."

"Aye, Ma'am. I apologize for letting my temper overrun my good sense." Cal stood at attention.

"Very well, Commander. We expect to see our city from the air for our Summer Ball. Are We clear? You've been given extraordinary power; We expect results to match."

"Your Majesty, I will obey your wish if I have to build the ship with my own hands." Cal went to her knee. "I will serve you and my country with my life. In everything, I am yours to command."

"Most commendable, We are touched by your fervour. Believe it or not, We were once young like you." The Queen stood. "Please forgive Our son. He changed his mind about putting you in command of your own security when you placed yourself between him and harm. He is alive because of you, We will not forget it."

Cal opened the door and the Queen swept out, pulling the prince and the Admiralty in her wake. Her Majesty paused at the top of the stairs.

"Since you are taking responsibility for security here, We expect you to keep yourself fully cognizant of the issues facing our great nation."

"Understood, Ma'am."

***

"Despite our agents' best efforts, we haven't been able to determine who funded the building of the fan engine. However, we have conclusive evidence that its design was based on plans stolen from the Shed. Commander Shillingsworth examined the plans used to construct the engine and found that other changes were made in the plans which made the thing even more unstable. We are now treating it as an assassination attempt on his Highness." Admiral of Intelligence McAllen sat down and waited for questions.

"I have been hearing some disturbing rumours." The Lord Admiral looked nervously at Cal. "They suggest she has a... close relationship with the ambassador from the Kershian Empire."

"Do they mention her friendship with the assistant to the Ambassador of the Zithayan Dynasty?" Cal leaned back against the wall. "Relax, I am aware of the talk. University students are always up to date on all the latest gossip."

"What do you plan to do about these lies?" The Lord Admiral looked nonplussed at Cal's lack of concern.

"Nothing." Cal sighed and leaned forward. "The more that I or any of you deny the rumours, the more credence some people will give them. If we ignore them, they will vanish with the next supposed scandal."

"And if they don't?" Vice-Admiral Peysk asked pointedly.

"If they outlast the usual gossip," Admiral McAllen tapped his fingers on the table, "then we can safely assume they are being spread deliberately. Either as an attack on Commander Shillingsworth, who is not without her enemies, or an attack on the project, hoping we will waste our time with doubt and extra layers of security."

Cal suppressed a grin. She'd only just learned that McAllen and Peysk were the only two to vote against limiting her command.

"We may be able to turn this to our advantage." McAllen looked over at Cal. "Though it may be uncomfortable for the Commander. If we act as if we believe the accusations, we may be able to draw out the people responsible."

"How uncomfortable do you plan on making it?" Cal raised an eyebrow. "I don't want anything to get in the way of my work."

"Nothing to interfere with the project, but a rather...inept tail put on you in public places."

"Meaning I will need to go to public places." Cal sighed. "I'm uncomfortable already." The others laughed. "We could go a step further if you think it would force the issue."

"You're thinking of meeting openly with the Ambassador." McAllen rolled his eyes. "It would certainly force the issue. You'd have to be careful to keep the occasions diplomatic. The gossips won't need anything more than the two of you in the same room to go into a frenzy."

"Since I don't keep track of such things, a list of events the Ambassador might attend would be helpful."

"If you're sure."

"I'd like to smoke them out and then smother the flames." Cal frowned. "While I'm prepared to ignore the gossip, I can't pretend it doesn't bother me."

"Very well," the Lord Admiral said, rising to leave. "We will let you and McAllen plot."

****

Cal walked back to the Shed with Bundo and Chief Petty Officer O'Brien flanking her.

"I'm still having problems understanding why I'm working for you," O'Brien muttered.

"You've demonstrated you can obey orders. If you obey me in that same fashion, we'll get along well. You also know the people and set up. I don't want to waste time training a new person."

"Aye, Ma'am. Thanks, I think..."

Cal walked into the shed and asked Bundo to whistle. She covered her ears before the piercing sound echoed through the cavernous space.

The engineers finished what they were doing and gathered around Cal.

"O'Brien, close the doors." Cal waited until they were shut and barred.

"Here's the plan." Cal put her hands behind her back to keep from waving them. "For reasons unrelated to our work here, you are going to hear a lot of nasty gossip if you haven't already." A few heads nodded. "I'm ordering you not contradict them with any vigour. There is a purpose for my request, and I'm going to ask you to trust me. If someone approaches you with a request which makes you uncomfortable, you are to discreetly report it to Chief Petty Officer O'Brien. At the same time, I want you to sound frustrated at our slow progress. Again, I'm not going to explain. Any questions?"

"Only the ones you said you're not answering," Landers said. The others shook their heads.

"Right then, back to work. We're working on a schedule now. Team leaders, in my office in five."

Cal climbed the stairs to her office. Tallinan was setting a tray with tea on her desk as she entered.

"Thank you, but that isn't necessary."

"You're my Commander." Tallinan returned to his office next door.

The team leads assembled.

"Progress reports."

"We've pushed the pressure on the boiler as far as we can without making it too heavy. A layer of insulating wrap is keeping the heat and pressure

up longer. It will mean a longer lead to get steam."
Digney shrugged. "Everything is a trade-off."

"The propellers are at peak efficiency. They're a balance between starting power and cruising. The oak is heavy but the most durable, even better than steel." Landers nodded in Digney's direction.

"We've moved away from trying to maximize the pressure through the fan engine." Patrick's fingers brushed the new Engineer Second Class emblem on his jacket. "The new goal is sustainable power. One of the guys has built a valve to top out the feed pressure well below the critical safety level. The biggest issue now is the fan engine heating up. When we run it too long, the fans scrape the casing."

"Give the fans more clearance."

"Aye, Ma'am." Patrick looked at her. "The system to direct the steam where we want it steals a little power, but that captured steam might be useful for heat or running small engines."

"Good notion," Cal approved.

"We've settled on a mix between a full frame on the envelope and none. We don't think the bag will take enough pressure to remain stiff in a rough wind. The more pressure, the less lifting power. There will be a full loop lengthwise of laminated wood for strength and lightness. A few hoops between bow and stern to help fasten the separate envelopes. If we lose one, it won't be catastrophic. We're thinking ladders to aid in repair and a rail for rappelling ropes to cover the areas not accessible by ladder." Ensign Cesare waved his hands to show the shapes he talked about. "With the decision on having a partial frame, we've been able to design the steering and stabilizers. They will need to work by cable, but I'm told the gondola will be toward the stern, so it will be doable. Speaking of the gondola, we are using the lamination idea to make strong surfaces without getting too heavy. With Patrick's idea of using waste steam for heat, we won't need as much insulation.

"Sounds good, we need to start coordinating so the gondola team knows where to build the engine room and the envelope has space for control cables." Cal looked around the room. "It is even more important now that all drawings and plans be stored in the secure room when not in use. Don't worry about being a bother, asking Chief O'Brien or me for access. Anything which is not put into the secure room is to be burned. I do not want a repeat of the disaster with the fan engine out there."

"Aye, Ma'am," they chorused and stood up.

"Dismissed."

# Chapter 12  - The Dangerous Game

Crysabel and her maid helped Cal into yet another new gown. At the rate she was spending money on clothes, the twenty thousand sovereign gift might hurt more than she thought. Who knew being wealthy was so expensive?

"Matilde, check the drape on your side." Crysabel huffed as she leaned forward to tug on the over blouse. This one was a green which reminded Cal of seaweed.

"When can I start wearing gowns I already own?" Cal twisted her neck to look at herself in the mirror. This made the fifth outing in a month.

"Oh, you can't do that." Crysabel clucked her tongue and made a microscopic adjustment. "People will start gossiping that you are going bankrupt."

"I'm filling a closet with gowns I will never likely wear again; I will be going bankrupt. Besides, I'm trying to encourage gossip that I might be traitor, a little chin-wagging about me being poor is the least of my worries."

"The people who invite you to these balls are milking the fascination with a high-ranking female naval officer who may or may not have an improper relationship with the Kershian Ambassador. That is interesting. Poverty is boring, they will worry you will try to hit them up for money. It's what they would do."

"Can we combine different gowns to make them look new?"

Crysabel looked thoughtful. Matilde nodded once.

"The coach will be here at any moment, my Lady."

Cal sighed and let Matilde help put her shoes on. They were so uncomfortable Cal insisted on putting them on last. She would have ridden to the ball and put them on in the carriage, but the gown didn't give her space to move.

Her live-in students lined up, leaning against the walls to watch her come down the stairs. *If I charged admission for these evenings, I could easily pay for the gown.* Pentam gazed up the stairs with a dazed look, but his eyes were focused over Cal's shoulder on Crysabel who was due to give birth to their first child at any time.

Bundo opened the door and helped Cal into the coach. He climbed up beside the driver and they were off.  Only in her own bedroom was Cal free of his presence. She'd thought having him as a shadow would be irritating, but she found it was a comfort.

"Your prey is in sight," Bundo whispered as he handed Cal out of the coach. "I saw the Kershian coach pull out as we came in."

"Thanks, I was despairing of anything coming of this. I could have used the time in the barn."

"Hans and I have been following your instructions. It may be time to ask Mr. Booksdale how to get the hydrogen."

"We are further along than I thought." Cal fussed with her gown to give her time to talk with Bundo.

"That much hydrogen will take time to assemble."

"True." Cal squared her shoulders. "Off to battle."

Bundo grinned and headed for the servant's entrance where he could be useful and entertaining, and not-coincidentally, close to the ballroom.

"The Lady Commander Calliope Shillingsworth."

Cal stepped through the doors as she was announced. Some bright soul had apparently decided Lady Commander was a proper title. She suspected the story of her temper tantrum had a lot to do with it. Cal smiled and floated across the floor as Crysabel had taught her.

A cluster of people made sure to cross her path and probe for any new rumours. Bri stood by the table helping himself to wine from a servant's tray. Cal timed her arrival to take the glass from his hand. Bri smiled and took another glass for himself.

"The famous Lady Commander herself." Bri toasted her. "It is true the Queen came and left the Admiralty on their knees while she dressed them down?"

"I think her Majesty was annoyed at the implication a woman wasn't fit for command."

"Understandable, but what price did you pay for the show?"

"She mentioned Arctic patrols if I repeated the performance." Cal sipped at her wine as they wandered from the table to meander through the crowd.

Bri laughed. "Your Queen is not to be trifled with; her name makes empires tremble."

Cal introduced Bri to some of her acquaintances as they passed. He answered questions about his homeland briefly and politely. The rest of the evening Cal kept the conversation light and away from politics. He could talk on anything from music to art, naming the piece the orchestra played or commenting on the paintings on the wall.

When the dancing began, Cal thought Bri might stay for a dance, but he dragged himself away reluctantly.

At least once a week, Cal arranged to 'bump' into the ambassador. She even went so far as attending concerts and galleries mid-week when she had the energy after work. She had Bundo drive her past the Embassy and took note of the Kershian guards inside the gate and Anglian on the outside.

***

"Why do you need ten thousand cubic yards of hydrogen?" Pentam met her at the door after a concert. "Trying to source that much at one time will raise eyebrows."

"Is there any way to do it without causing suspicion?"

"We could make it ourselves." Pentam shook his head. "Produce it through electrolysis from water.. All we would need is the water itself and sufficient electricity."

"I know a guy who invented this electrical engine thing which can make electricity," she commented helpfully.

"You'll want a way of turning the magnet."

"Gowns are a mystery beyond me, but making something spin, that I can do."

She, Pentam, Hans and Bundo spend a week of evenings setting up the system to split hydrogen from the water. Cal made a chute to capture the hydrogen from the barrel of water as it bubbled up and deliver the gas to the envelope. The fan engine on low pressure turned the magnet as fast as Cal thought safe. Very slowly the envelope took shape. Lacking a rigid frame on her airship, she used nets from fishing boats to hold the gondola to the envelope.

***

Bedlam greeted her as Cal walked into the house. The students paced nervously with Pentam in the parlour. Crysabel was in her room accompanied by

Matilde and the midwife. The sounds of her labour floated down the stairs.

"Sorry, my lady, but I've been busy so with helping Lady Crysabel; I haven't had time to think of supper." Beth wrung her hands.

"I'm sure the students have raided kitchens before, they'll have to fend for themselves." Cal glanced over at Pentam who looked ready to faint. "I'll get one of them to take care of Pentam."

A knock on the door sent Cal back to open it as she waved at Beth to do whatever she needed.

Hyansea stood on the step. That's right, she sent a card asking to visit.

"Come in and welcome." Cal stepped back. "But the house is in chaos, as my dear friend is giving birth to her first child. I won't be insulted if you decide to return another day."

"No, I would be honoured to join your chaos." She called something to her driver in a language which sounded half song. The driver bowed and drove away. "La will bring some things from the embassy. We will help you to celebrate as we do in Zithaya."

"The parents-to-be will be delighted." Cal led Hyansea to the parlour. "Pentam, you remember Hyansea. I forgot I'd invited her tonight. She is going to help you celebrate the birth in the Zithayan fashion."

"Welcome, welcome, Crysabel will be so excited." Pentam took a couple of steps toward the stairs, then stopped. He looked at Cal with panicked eyes. "Can you take the message, I, I can't go up there."

Cal hugged him, "of course." She climbed the stairs, not much less nervous than Pentam. A gentle knock brought Matilde to the door of Crysabel and Pentam's suite, her father's old rooms.

"My Lady, the birth is going as expected and the young mother is doing well."

"I will take the news to Pentam. He wanted you to let Crysabel know the Zithayan assistant ambassador is here and planning to celebrate the birth as they do in Zithaya."

Matilde looked doubtful but went back into the room. She returned less than a minute later.

"Lady Crysabel is ecstatic. If she isn't able to travel to the world, the world is coming to her." The door closed again and Cal took the news down to Pentam and Hyansea.

More than an hour later, a knock announced La's return. He brought three women with him who carried baskets in. The students ran to fetch tables to put them on while exotic odours wafted from the baskets. La carried a box which he set beside Hyansea. The women uncovered the baskets and laid out a feast.

Cal's stomach growled, Hyansea laughed and led Cal to the table and filled a plate for her. The students followed and even Pentam took a small plate. Hans and Bundo appeared and joined in. When they'd made a sizable dent in the food, Hyansea opened the box and took out a tiny bottle.

"This is a special wine for new fathers, to calm them." She pulled out a clay cup, opened the bottle and poured it carefully, emptying every drop.

Pentam took the drink cautiously and sniffed at it like a brandy. His eyes widened and he took a sip.

"Cal, I'd offer you a taste, but Hyansea said it is for the fathers." He drank again and sighed.

Hyansea dug into the box again and took out a red silk cloth. It had a tiger embroidered on it. The beast looked ready to leap from the fabric. She handed it to Pentam.

"When it is time, wrap your child in this. Year of the Tiger, very good luck."

Pentam ran his fingers across the square of cloth. Hyansea smiled and put two tiny figurines on the table, each fastened to a fine chain.

"This one if a girl." She pointed to one. "And this if a boy. Give to the mother of your child for good spirits." Hyansea closed the box and folded her hands on her lap. "We wait and send health and strength to the mother." She closed her eyes. Cal copied her and saw most of the others do the same before she closed her eyes.

Crysabel had become her dearest friend, there at Cal's father's funeral and here to help make Cal into a lady. She almost snorted. All that time she'd spent fighting against it, and her friend accomplished the impossible with humour and grace. Encouraging her and Pentam to meet ranked among her best ideas. They were so madly happy; it scared Cal a little. What would it be like to feel that?

The sounds upstairs changed, and soon after Matilde appeared on the stairs, a grin on her face and tears in her eyes.

"My Lady is doing fine. As are your children."

"Children?" Pentam put a hand out to steady himself.

"Twins, Mr. Booksdale. A girl and a boy."

Hyansea clapped her hands and said something in her liquid language. La and the women from the Embassy bowed deeply to Pentam twice, then broke into a song which tugged at Cal's heart. Hyansea opened the box to pull out another blanket, this one black with a fearsome tiger roaring embroidered on it. La handed Hyansea a lacquered tray. She put the figurines on the tray along with a bowl of clear broth.

"For mother, to make her strong."

Pentam put the cloths over his arm and picked up the tray to follow Matilde up the stairs. He had a smile on his face which looked like it would never leave.

A short while later, Pentam and Matilde came down the stairs each carrying a tiny bundle wrapped in silk.

"Meet Andrew." Pentam lifted the baby wrapped in the black cloth, "and Calli." Matilde lifted her bundle in red. "Crysabel wanted to name her Calliope, but I told her you threatened violence, so we shortened it. It is all right?"

Cal opened her mouth to reply with some smart remark, but to her horror tears flowed from her eyes and words couldn't pass the lump in her throat. Matilde handed Cal the infant girl. She vaguely knew the Zithayans were singing again. The students were trying to join it to the amusement of all. Pentam was saying something to Hyansea.

Cal's entire world had shrunk to the tiny perfect girl in her arms.

"I will teach you to draw, to build things, to sail the oceans. Whatever there is in the world I can give is yours." Cal whispered and ran her finger across the incredibly soft skin on Calli's brow.

***

"I hear congratulations are in order." Bri handed Cal a glass of water as they milled with the crowd waiting for intermission to end. "I am happy to hear of such joy. I remember my daughter's birth." A flash of pain crossed his eyes. "She is so like her mother, but I don't get to see her often enough. If only her mother could have watched her grow up." He drank from his wine glass and closed his eyes for a moment. "My apologies, I should not be bringing my pain into your joy."

"Pain is part of life, too." Cal put her hand on his arm briefly.

"In any case, I have a small token for your friends' children." He reached into a pocket to bring out two small velvet bags. Opening one, he dumped out a crystal cut in innumerable facets.

"My hometown is famous for its crystal. Hang these in a window and the room will be filled with rainbows." He put the crystal back in the bag and handed them to Cal.

"Why don't you come by and deliver them yourself?" She held the surprisingly heavy bags in her hand.

"I cannot." Bri put his glass down. "I am risking too much already." He looked at Cal. "You won't let me go. I can't..." He bowed over her hand and left, leaving a wake of whispers behind him.

Cal hefted the crystals, and for some unfathomable reason felt like crying.

***

She didn't see Bri for a week, forcing herself to make small talk and not scan the room for his rugged face. When he did show up, a blonde woman in an elegant dress on his arm, his eyes paused briefly on Cal's face before sliding along

Toward the end of the evening, Bri crossed paths with Cal.

"Lady Shillingsworth, meet Sigrid. She is newly arrived at the embassy and wanted to see the town." He bowed over her hand as Sigrid frowned at him. She dragged him away before Cal could say a word.

It was just as well. The tiny piece of paper in her hand shocked her beyond speaking.

Cal greeted a few more people then wandered to the washroom. The message sent cold down her spine as she read it.

Your life's in danger. Not my people.

Cal crumpled the paper and sent it down the drain. Then she went back out to mingle until she could safely leave without revealing the panic churning in her gut.

"This is why I guard you," Bundo said when she sat to talk with him in the barn. The envelope had begun to take shape.

"It's more the risk he took to warn me." Cal shook her head. "I wouldn't be surprised if Sigrid is here to get him under control. I knew I was playing with fire, but I never imagined it could burn him."

"He is an old hand at this." Bundo stretched. "A warrior with many scars to his honour. Don't discount that he is also playing the game."

"I won't." Despite her words, Cal had trouble sleeping. Bri's face haunted her. Not the polished mask with Sigrid at his side, but the anguished, trapped look she'd seen in his eyes before he ran away from her at the concert.

# Chapter 13   - Keep your enemy closer

Cal walked in the door to her home to find Hyansea drinking tea in the parlour with Crysabel. The twins slept nearby in cradles.

"I took the liberty of bringing my own tea." Hyansea poured into a cup and handed it to Cal. "I will leave some for you."

Beth brought in a tray with scones and jam and put it beside Hyansea.

"If I could bring the secrets of these home, my rank would go up at least two grades." Hyansea spread jam on one and bit into it with a sigh.

"I'm sure I could teach you how to make them," Beth said. "They aren't difficult once you have the knack."

"In the name of cultural exchange." Hyansea's eyes lit up. "In some part of the Dynasty there is a growing interest in western food. Not everyone agrees, but I think eating food from another country helps one to understand better."

"I wouldn't mind learning some of the dishes you brought to the babes' birth. The students have been asking if I could cook something like them."

"Perhaps a trade." Hyansea gazed into the distance." Sadly, I don't have time myself to learn to cook your food. I barely can cook Zithayan food as it is. Crysabel, I have been giving thought to Pentam and your visit to Zithaya. It might be wise to have you learn something about the culture before you come. It would be unfortunate to mar your time with a mistaken insult. Perhaps I could attach a couple of people to your home to teach them something of the way of our society. They would be able to take time to trade skills in the kitchen at the same time."

"That sounds like a wonderful idea." Crysabel picked up Andrew, who'd begun to fuss. "The young men in the room down the hall are moving out. Seems they have a trip they are taking with their class. Our visitors from the Embassy could stay there. It will be a way to keep Pentam from obsessing on his dissertation presentation. He could defend it in his sleep, but he's so sure he's missing things."

"I think it is a lovely idea." Cal sipped at the tea. A different taste than the one she'd been given on the ship, but just as good. "Hyansea, may I leave it up to you and Crysabel to work out the details?"

"Most certainly." Hyansea took another scone and smiled.

*** 

"Captain," Bundo stopped her in the hall. "There are people watching the house. At least two groups. One I expect is the Naval Intelligence people intended to be visible. The others are very good, but only have a rotation of three men. I expect the second group is aware of the navy, but it is hard to say if the reverse is true."

"What do you suggest?"

"We should increase the security of the house."

"True." Cal rubbed her temple. "But if the security on the place suddenly increases, it will tell them we know they are there, and more, there is something here worth looking for."

"You're suggesting we need a covert response." Bundo pursed his lips thoughtfully. "Guards who don't look like guards."

"I have an idea about that."

Cal found Pentam in the parlour.

"There are four students going on this expedition. They'll be gone for several months." Pentam swirled his wine and sighed. "It will be too quiet without them. That's a third of the students living with us. I'll have to mention at the university there are spaces available."

"One room will be taken by the people from the Zithayan embassy who'll be giving you cultural pointers and some language lessons. But the other one..." Cal trailed off and stared into the fire.

"Cal, are you all right?" Pentam leaned over and put a hand on her shoulder. "You've been pushing yourself hard with the engineering and the cloak and dagger stuff."

"Right. I'm fine." Cal shook herself. "Leave it to me. You worry about your dissertation and getting ready to go and impress Zithaya."

"Sure, if you insist." He frowned doubtfully but didn't pursue the matter.

***

The next morning at the Shed, Cal walked through the main floor with O'Brien and new guard who looked no different than any of the others on

O'Brien's squad but was a liaison to McAllen in intelligence.

"We use the main doors for everything." Cal stood looking out through the open double doors. "Steam carriages and wagons can park beside the doors and even drive into the Shed if needed. There are two other exits on the main floor." She walked across the large space. "This door in the back corner is nailed shut, probably to keep explorers out when this was empty space. We've left it blocked. It's too close to the fail test area for it to be safely used. It should be regularly checked at night to be sure no one's been messing with it."

Cal climbed the stairs to the second level and walked to the end of the hall, leading them through a door into a room on the right, which had an outside wall. "This one was blocked with shelving and debris." She pointed to a door that sported a hand-wheel. "I had the guys fabricate a steel door. It's locked with a version of the dogs on a ship's hatch. Steel bars run into the wall top and bottom. There's no way to open it from the outside. There was a rickety staircase, which we replaced it with a ladder. This is an emergency-only exit. It should be checked, but nothing short of a bomb will open it from the outside. If someone were going to use explosives, they'd be better to attack a wall directly."

"That takes care of people coming in through doors. What about the windows?" The 'guard' asked.

"Two windows. One is in my office and another in a meeting room. Neither opens. They've been painted shut."

"So, we can watch for people leaving the building by monitoring the doors and windows. What if someone opened the hatch and passed out a package?"

Cal turned the hand-wheel and pulled the door open. The hinges screeched, making O'Brien wince.

"I still have a hard time believing you did that purposefully." O'Brien looked out the door and waved at someone.

"The door opens toward the main path between the Academy building and the checkpoint at the gate. There are always people walking there. We've yet to open the thing without having someone wave at us."

"Good." The other man nodded to himself. "We should be able to keep you secure, and prevent any theft of plans."

"That's the idea." Cal led the way back to her office where Bundo sat in a chair in the corner reading a book.

"Tallinan is out at the moment, so no tea. The stove is in his office."

"Not a problem. Now that I've been oriented to the place, I know where I need to put my men."

"I'd like to you to take a message to Admiral McAllen for me." Cal leaned against one of her tables. "Tell him I have space in my house for two 'students'."

"Understood." He smiled faintly.

Cal saw O'Brien and the liaison man out of her office and went to work. She was trying to create an overall plan for the airship so they could spot holes in the design. The sheet she worked on was in fact several sheets glued together, large enough to cover an entire table top. Even then some of the details were too small to show and several supplementary drawings covered the other tables.

The amount of progress they'd made was encouraging, but the road ahead was still a long one. One of the biggest challenges would be sourcing the amount of cloth they needed for the envelope and the hydrogen to fill it. She'd get

Tallinan to put out feelers. The sooner they had those things in hand the better.

"Time to go, Captain." Bundo stood up and stretched.

"Right," Cal put her pencil down and stood back to look at the drawing. It looked like an airship. She felt an echo of her awe at seeing the Ferandican airship the first time. "Help me roll these up and put them in the file room." They tidied up Cal's office. She picked up the rolls of plans the teams had put in the box outside her office.

All of it locked securely away, Cal followed Bundo out to the steam carriage. The guards outside the Shed door secured it and double checked.

"Have a good evening, Commander," one said.

"Thank you."

Bundo opened the steam valve and they chugged away through the gate. Cal watched to see which way he would take home this time. There were only two places they had to pass on every trip. One was a bridge. Taking a different bridge would add an hour to the trip. The other was the last stretch of road to the house.

"You must have spent every day since we got here exploring the city."

"A hunter must know the ground." Bundo tilted his head toward a building. "That is the only building on this block with an outside ladder to the roof. All the others have trap doors from the attic space." He pointed his chin at one on the other side of the street. "That one has access to the sewers from the basement."

"I'm impressed." Cal looked around. "I need to start paying a lot more attention to these things."

"Perhaps; you have me to watch for you." He swung around a corner. "If you spent too much time trying to learn the lay of the land, you wouldn't have time to do your work." As the carriage rattled around another corner, Bundo slowed to examine the bridge and the entry to it. "Hold on, something is wrong."

"Do we take the long way around?"

"Don't have enough steam." Bundo thumped the wheel. "Hans is waiting on a part to fix a leak. A trap we know about is one we can reverse. Be ready to move if I say."

To Cal's puzzlement, Bundo trundled onto the bridge slower than he usually took it. The paving was rough and she normally had to hang on tight. A steam carriage zoomed out of an alley and blocked the bridge behind them. A horse-drawn wagon pulled across the exit. Bundo braked and cut the steam.

"Watch the rear," Bundo said. "Let me know how many come at us." He handed her a tangle of ropes. "I'm told you know how to use this."

Cal kept her eyes scanning the bridge as she sorted out the harness and put it on.

"There's a coil of rope already fastened to the car. Grab hold and get ready."

She found the rope and checked the knot attaching it to the carriage. There was a clip on the rope. Moving it to her harness to attach the rope to her took only seconds.

"Four coming from the rear. Looks like they have clubs rather than knives or guns."

"Six from the front. Get ready." Bundo leaned forward to take hold of a lever she hadn't noticed before. "When I say go, throw the rope over the portside railing and go over with it. There's a boat moored below us. Get in the boat. Wait for me there."

The men ran from both directions, spreading out across the width of the bridge to leave no space to escape.

They were no more than ten feet from the carriage when Bundo pulled the lever. With a loud hiss, steam poured out from beneath the carriage, hitting the cold stone of the bridge and making an instant fog.

"Go."

Cal heaved the rope over the railing, then rolled over to stand on the outside of the bridge. She rappelled down the pillar to a few feet above the river. A ledge ran around the base of the pillar. Her feet on the ledge she hugged the stone and sidled around to the boat and climbed in, then unclipped from the rope. Shouts and curses came from above, then a splash told her someone had gone over the side. Bundo surfaced beside the boat and rolled into it.

"Wait." He held up his hand. A sharp bang echoed off the warehouses on either side of the river. "Let's go." He took one oar, Cal the other as she cast off. They'd hardly cleared the shadow of the bridge when a much louder bang sounded. The second blast blew the fog away from the bridge, showing Cal the steam carriage burning while a few men fled with hands up, shielding their heads. None of them took time to look over at the river. Another thump sounded as the boiler blew, sending another cloud of steam out. Bundo had them pull into a tiny slip a few minutes' row downstream.

He climbed out of the boat and led the way through back alleys to a road where they could hire a cab.  He seemed about as rattled by the turn of events as if Beth had announced she was making shepherd's pie instead of chicken pot pie for supper.

Hans met them in the yard, looking curiously at their dishevelled states.

"Problems with the steam carriage?"

"You could say that." Cal led the way to the house. "First thing, Bundo, get dried off and dry clothes on. Meet me in the parlour."

***

"It looked more like an attempt to capture than kill." Bundo drank his tea and nibbled the sweets on a plate left by Beth. "They had a plan, but no backup. Someone should have been sent back to watch for exactly the kind of trick we used."

"What would you have done if they'd had guns?"

"Taken them away, made them regret their stupidity." Bundo stared into his tea. "We won't be able to use the same trick again. Next time they'll be ready and won't close in. Our response will need to change."

"I can ask for an escort to and from the Academy." Cal put her tea down and poured herself a glass of brandy. "An attack on a

Commander demands a heavy-handed response. The advantage will be you can shadow us and see who is planning what. Whatever they want, I don't think a pitched battle in the city is part of their plans."

"Very well. I'd suggest you send a messenger immediately."

***

The Navy Coach and the twenty-man squad made the trip to and from the Shed safer, but slower. Cal took to bringing her sketchbook in the coach to give herself something to do. The guard at the Shed doubled.

Bundo reported that no one followed them, or observed from anywhere he could see.

Cal still went out to social events, not as frequently as before, but to her surprise, she enjoyed the chance to talk with people about things which had little connection to anything important. She occasionally saw Bri, always with Sigrid on his arm. He made sure he never got close enough to talk to Cal.

Early in October, Cal was invited to a masked ball. It wasn't a family who asked her before, but she'd spoken to them on occasion. It sounded like fun. Crysabel plotted with Hyansea to have Cal go in Zithayan Dynasty clothing.

The outfit looked gorgeous, a deep red, with a serpent embroidered on the hems and cuffs. The shoes for the thing looked uncomfortable, but Cal thought them better than the slippers she'd had to wear with the gowns. The only drawback was the outfit was more restrictive than any of the gowns Cal owned.

"You must walk slowly with small steps. You are too important to rush." Hyansea coached her on how to act.

On the day of the ball, Crysable, Hyansea and Nyian, the Zithayan woman who lived in the house as a language teacher, worked together to stuff Cal into the dress and put on the layers of makeup which went with the outfit.

Bundo had to lift her into the coach, where Cal sat stiffly, afraid to move and put anything out of place. Nyian rode with her to repair any damage. Bundo lifted Cal out, then Nyian inspected the outfit and gave her approval.

As a masked ball, people weren't announced. Whispers went around the room when Cal walked into the room with her tiny slow steps. To add to the effect, she used her very small store of Zithayan words to greet people.

The buzz followed her all evening. Cal found she didn't mind that eating and drinking looked to be more difficult in her new outfit.

Nobody had thought about what she needed to do if she had to use the washroom. Cal didn't think she could get *out* of the clothes by herself, never mind get back *into* them. In desperation, she cornered one of the maids serving the guest and asked her to take a message to Nyian who'd be waiting with Bundo near the kitchen.

Cal headed down the long hallway away from the ballroom, following the maid's directions. Nyian would meet her there. Walking with such small steps was exhausting. Cal briefly considered making an early exit, only she was sure Hyansea would be disappointed.

The bag over her head almost sent her tumbling, but strong arms lifted her and jogged away. The dress bound her as efficiently as ropes. The dust from the sac made her cough until the world spun around her. Cal thought she been put in a wagon, but she couldn't say for sure.

She lay concentrating on breathing without coughing and thinking through her predicament. Whoever had grabbed her wanted something. If they'd intended her death, she'd be a corpse in the river already.

Rough hands dragged her out of wherever she was and carried her into a house, and down the stairs. She was dumped into a chair and her hands tied behind her. Then she waited, the dampness working its way through the sac, chilling her.

"My, my," the voice made Cal grind her teeth. She only knew one person who could make innocuous words sound like an insult. "How far the great Shillingsworth family has fallen, pretending to be a foreign whore. Of course, we both know it isn't far from the truth." A blow rocked her head and almost knocked her to the floor. "You've stolen from me, insulted me, made me look bad in front of my peers."

"You didn't need any help from me to achieve that last part."

The blow to her stomach took the wind from her and left Cal gasping.

"Since you insist on talking like a man I will oblige." Another blow pushed her out of the chair to land on the floor.

"I'm tired," Cal said. "I'd like nothing better than a bath, so get to the point. Unless you did all this just to show how manly you are by beating up someone bound and blinded."

Someone picked her up and slammed her back into her chair.

"Fine, since you are so impatient." A hand grabbed the bag and twisted, cutting off her air. "You stole my future. That electrical machine was my retirement. I would finally have been able to live as I deserved."

Cal wanted to taunt him more but didn't have the breath to talk.

"You will hand over plans to this airship you're building. They'll be worth more than that machine. Do this and I'll even let you live in your fantasy where people think you're important. You're a tool, nothing more, but I'll allow you to learn it for yourself. I know you think you're brave and not afraid of death, but what about those people around you? Your friends and their precious babies? Infants are so fragile, and I'll make sure they know it was your choice. You choose yourself over them. I have evidence of your treason. The Shillingsworth name will never recover." He let go of the bag and Cal gasped in air. She tried to form words, but what came out was laughter. The situation was absurd. How could he believe any of this would sway her?

He hit her again and again, screaming obscenities at her. Finally, she lay on the floor retching, thankful she hadn't anything to eat.

"If I walk out of this room, I will destroy everyone you care about."

"Fine." Cal spat out blood. "But even if I give you what you want, you'll still never be anything more than a spineless worm."

He growled.

"You kill me, you get nothing. The only way forward is to keep me alive. You aren't the only person after my skin. If one of them gets to me, you're done. So if you want your plans and wealth, you keep me alive until they're done."

"I can kill you and steal what you've already done."

"I'm the only one who can build this thing. Ask any of my engineers."

"You are to start sending me plans. Immediately. Leave them in your desk, my person will pick them up. Oh yes, I have someone in your group, I already know everything you're doing." He sneered and Cal bit her cheek to keep from laughing. How desperate he was to show his importance.

"Right, let me go have my bath, and your spy can build the thing for you." Cal lay on the floor, fog from the pain and lack of air making her detached from the world. She decided on a whimper to play to the man's ego. He needed to think he'd won.

Hands snatched her up and carried her out into the cold air. The wagon rolled through the streets. Cal concentrated on breathing, spitting out blood whenever it threatened to choke her. Someone yanked her out of the wagon and dropped her on the cobbled road. The ropes binding her hands vanished and the bag was pulled off her head. She couldn't get her eyes to focus on the vague shape walking away. The clop of hooves and creak of wheels faded.

Cal lay on her back staring up into the black sky. Somehow she needed to find the strength to get up and walk somewhere, anywhere, to get help. It just wasn't there.

A face leaned over her, it faded in and out of focus.

"Bri," Cal whispered. "What...?"

"Hush." Bri put a finger on her lips, then picked her up. "Let me take you somewhere safe." He carried her through silent streets until they got to a park, the trees looming bare and stark over her. Bri laid her on a bench, then wrapped a coat around her.

"Someone will come soon. Just wait for them. You're safe. I swear it. I will find out who did this and kill him."

"Not yet," Cal whispered. She closed her eyes and waited for someone to come and take her home to hot water and safety.

# Chapter 14  - Turncoat

Cal shivered staring up at the gaslight. Had Bri really been there? If he'd been there, why had he left her alone in the cold and dark? She wanted to sit up, to move, but she barely had the strength to breathe. Her ribs hurt again, so did her face. Crysabel would be so angry at her.

"Captain?" Someone shook her gently. "Captain?"

Cal opened her eyes, but couldn't focus them. Even blurred she knew it was Bundo leaning over her.

"I knew you'd come."

He swept her up and carried her to the coach, laying her on the seat before climbing up to drive.

"Sorry, my lady, but I must see the extent of your injuries." Nyian brushed a featherlight hand across Cal's brow. "Bruises, no cuts." The woman's hand pressed on Cal's stomach as impersonal as the wind. "No bleeding inside." She tilted Cal's face to one side, then the other with a gentle finger. "You will show the marks on your face, but no bones are broken."

"Spitting blood." Cal rasped, trying not to cough.

"Your lip is split." Nyian wrapped Cal in soft fabric.

At the house, Bundo carried her in and straight up the stairs.

"Bath," Cal whispered into his chest.

"Nyian will set the water to heat."

"No reason to wait." Cal closed her eyes. "Use steam to keep water hot all the time. Can even pump it through the house."

"For now, you wait. Tomorrow is soon enough to tear the house apart."

"Remind me," Cal asked. "If I forget tomorrow. Steam to heat water."

"I'll tell you, Captain."

Beth and Nyian came in with buckets to fill the tub and soon there was enough steaming water for Bundo to lower Cal, blanket and all, into the water. He left her with Beth and Nyian.

"I put oils in the water to speed healing." Nyian opened a tiny bottle and poured something into the bath. The scent cut through the fog in Cal's head and eased the aches from her body.

Someone was washing Cal's hair. She relaxed and let herself be spoiled.

"Can you get out on your own?" Crysabel took Cal's hand.

"I think so." Cal hoisted herself up with the help of the other women and stepped out onto a soft rug. Beth wrapped her in a towel, while Nyian stood with a robe ready. They walked Cal to her room and tucked her into bed.

Part of Cal shook with fear. She wanted to clutch at her friends, keep them at her side, but exhaustion sent her to sleep before her hands could move.

***

Light from the window woke Cal. It had to be time, past time, for her to get to work, but her body refused to obey her commands.

"Ah, you're awake," Beth pushed herself out a chair. "My Lady you gave me a scare. Are you able to get up?"

With considerable hissing and a few curses which made Beth blush, Cal got out of bed, into a shift, and then a warm robe. Bundo waited outside the door to guide her down the stairs.

He helped her sit in a chair in the dining room and brought tea over to her.

"Beth will bring in breakfast in a minute." Bundo went to his knee beside her. "I failed you. I should have been there."

"No." Cal put her hand on his shoulder. "I suspected something like this might happen, perhaps worse." She closed her eyes and took stock of the damage. "I know it looks bad, but the prince did more damage saving my life." A grin pained her lip, so Cal kept her face straight. "We move to step two of the plan. You and two other people will be the only ones who can know. The trap is baited, now we wait while our quarry thinks he's hunting us."

"You know who it is."

"I do." Cal winced as the hot tea stung her lip. "I will write up a full report which you will keep safe in case of my death. It might not hang him, but it will force him into the light."

"Who?"

"I trust you with my life." Cal gazed at Bundo over her cup. "But I fear if I tell you, it will influence your actions. He cannot suspect he is prey, and not the predator."

"My captain." Bundo put his hand over his heart. "Command me."

"Very well. I need a message taken to the Shed informing them of the situation and that I will not be present for the rest of the week."

A police officer showed up mid-morning.

"Inspector Beshuin, my Lady." He bowed, then sat across from Cal when she waved him to a seat. "Sorry, my Lady, but I need to take a statement. Baroness Naismith is distraught that a guest was taken from her home. She wishes the perpetrators caught, horsewhipped, hung, then boiled in oil." The man smiled. "The Baroness is not someone whom I'd want angry at me."

"I understand." Cal sighed and winced at the twinge from her ribs. "But I will not be much help. They put a bag over my head so I saw nothing at all. Even after they cut the rope binding my arms and removed the bag, my eyes didn't focus quickly enough to say anything more than a shadow walking away."

"I heard the burned-out hulk of your steam carriage was found on the Chessop Bridge."

"We had a bit of trouble."

"The kind of trouble which leaves bodies behind." The Inspector looked sharply at Cal.

"I am not well-liked in some circles."

"Forgive me, my Lady, but dislike doesn't usually result in corpses and beatings."

"This is true, but the people involved have goals beyond the obvious." Cal closed her eyes and picked her words carefully. "You may know a bit of the work I am doing."

"I know you are introduced as the Lady Commander, have been linked in some minds with a certain Ambassador. The exact nature of your work is not my business."

"I would be surprised if you had. The people who work for me are sworn to secrecy. This project will turn the tide of the next war."

"You are suggesting this was an attempt to gain information from you."

"I think so, an attempt to scare me in preparation for such an attempt at the least." Cal sipped at her tea again. "Many think a woman too frail to withstand the fear of such an assault." She put her cup down a little more forcefully than necessary. "I have faced death before, and will again, but no kind of threat will convince me to betray my country."

"I see." The Inspector leaned back and eyed Cal for a long moment before he sighed. "I will file my report and leave the situation for your superiors to handle as they will."

"Perhaps, if you have an opportunity to see the Baroness, you could pass on my apology for being so rude as to be abducted from her ball. I was enjoying myself up to that point."

The Inspector laughed, then stood up and bowed slightly.

"Accept my hopes for a quick recovery." He handed her a card. "If you have the need of the police for any reason, contact me here."

Beth showed him out.

"I think I will sit in the parlour for a time." Cal looked at the card and sighed.

Bundo came from where he'd been sitting out of sight and walked beside her.

"Already, I feel stronger." Cal settled into her chair. "Beth's food is good medicine." She pulled out a notebook and began to write up the summary of events for Bundo to keep safe.

"My Lady, you have a caller. She apologizes for coming uninvited but wished to see for herself that you are well." Beth put her head in the door.

"If she doesn't mind that I'm not properly dressed to receive visitors, show her in."

Beth left and returned shortly leading Baroness Naismith.

"My dear Lady Shillingsworth, I am mortified."

"Beth, perhaps bring tea and leave us for a while.

***

When Cal walked through the doors into the Shed, Landers shouted "Commander on deck" and the engineers formed up to welcome her back.

"I'm touched," Cal said to them. "It's good to be back. Now, team leaders in my office in five. I want to know what you've been doing in my absence."

The day passed quickly. She added the new information to the large plan for the airship and several details to the small drawings. To get a solid feel for what the engineers had been doing, Cal pulled the clean copies of the plans from the locked room, then updated them with the new advances. She quickly made copies of the plans before putting the originals back into the locked room.

The escort from the Navy doubled, making the trip from the Academy to her house even slower. She was sure there were more watching the house. Cal passed the time with her sketchbook. At home, she met Hans in the stable to work on her plan to heat water and keep it hot.

"We don't need a high-pressure boiler." Cal tapped on the tank. "It only needs to hold the water at a hot temperature, not as steam. It will mean we don't need to watch the pressure beyond a release if the pressure gets too high."

"We'd be best to set it up in the shed outside the kitchen." Hans walked around the tank. "It will keep the fire hazard down and Beth uses more hot water than the baths."

"Sounds good." Cal sketched on a paper pinned to the wall. "We put the tank on feet and make space below it for the fire. Make an enclosure around the tank to the chimney. Keep the heat in as much as possible."

"I can get our usual man to make the necessary parts." Hans drew in a couple of lines. "If we put in a line here, we can pump water into the tank to replace what is used. By setting that up in the evening, it should be hot by morning."

"Good thinking." Cal rubbed her eyes carefully. The bruises on her face were still tender. "If this works, I expect we can make a fortune selling these. Father has left me interest in several manufacturing plants which could easily make this kind of thing."

"Do you need the money?" Hans lifted an eyebrow.

"Not really, but if I'm going to be giving away lots of money, it will be helpful to have more income."

"You are giving money away?"

"I suppose I haven't told you. Cameron about died when I told him I'd pledged 20,000 sovereigns to Prince Alfred's art museum project."

To his credit, Hans didn't pale a much as Cameron had, but then he wasn't an accountant.

"I see." Hans unpinned the plan. "I will see about getting the pieces we need made."

Cal meandered over to the barn to see the envelope had become almost taut. The little airship floated, held down by ropes at each corner. She climbed up the ladder to the gondola. It would be spacious for one, cramped for two. Adding her weight made the ship sink. Close, but not there yet.

***

"All right, crew. The moment has arrived." Cal looked over the gathered engineers. "We are going to start assembling a prototype airship. It won't be full scale, as it must fit within this building. I have the complete plan drawn out, with detailed illustrations where needed. I fully expect we will discover all kinds of things we should have thought of earlier. The important thing is to fix the issue and move forward. Let's not waste time with blame."

The engineers nodded and murmured to each other.

"The first order of business is to decide on the order in which the parts should be assembled. Once we start filling the envelope with hydrogen, there will be no flame or even sparks allowed in the Shed. No matter how we treat the fabric to be fireproof, the hydrogen will burn."

"If there is a fire, ring that bell." Cal pointed to the newly installed brass bell. "If you hear it, drop everything and get out. Use the main doors, or if you're upstairs the back hatch. Do not try to rescue anything. I will not trade lives for paper."

"Team leads, in my office in five to determine the construction order. The rest of you, check what we have on hand and give Petty Officer Tallinan a list of anything you need."

The ship began to take shape. The partial frame was hung from the ceiling, then the envelope stretched over it. The main keel for the gondola they laid on the floor beneath the envelope, then fastened the boiler, engine and shaft to it. They began to assemble the gondola around it, stringing cables which would steer the airship.

Each night Cal copied plans, locked one set in the room and hid the other in her desk. Sometime during the day, the extra plans disappeared.

***

"We should be able to test the prototype in the Shed before the end of the month. After that, we build another one outside and fly it in the open air."

"Excellent news." The Lord Admiral leaned back smiling. "What's next?"

"If all goes well, we build a full-size ship based on what we learn from the prototype. We will still have a lot to learn. Each time we scale up the machine, things will need to be changed."

"Very good. My daughter and her husband are visiting from Ferandica. The airship arrived this morning. I am looking forward to a ride on our own vessel." The prince grinned at Cal.

They went through the rest of the meeting.

"Your Highness, if I may have a word in private?" Cal waited for him at the door. The prince stepped back into the room and closed the door.

"I haven't had a proper chance to inquire after your health." The prince looked at Cal.

"That's part of what I wish to discuss," Cal said. "The situation is a little more complicated than I initially reported to the Admiralty..."

***

Cold winds made Cal fear they'd be too late in the season for a proper test of the prototype outside. The ship in the Shed was almost complete and hydrogen bubbled up into the envelope from four tanks. They'd accomplished everything they could until it lifted off and they could check the balance.

The small ship in her barn required weight on the bow to keep the nose down. The wings she'd attached, folded in against the gondola. They'd spread quickly with the turn of a winch. She'd tested the engine and it worked better than she'd expected. Instead of fastening a boiler with a fire to heat it, Cal bolted the sphere down hanging below the airship. She'd had Hans order a shield so she could heat the boiler without risk of lighting the hydrogen on fire.

Cal walked around the Shed giving one last inspection to the work done that day. All that remained were details. The ship would indeed fly. It floated on taut ropes below, slack ropes above which had held the weight of the envelope. She had to make her notes for the day and finish the plans.

"O'Brien. Give me an hour, then have the escort ready." Bundo followed her upstairs. Tallinan still worked in his office.

"Working late, Petty Officer?" Cal stuck her head in his door.

"Aye, Commander. All this work has created a mountain of paperwork. The Navy likes to have every penny accounted for."

"I'll be done in an hour. You have until then."

"I should be able to finish in time."

Cal went to her office and got to work. She put the plans in the locked room and inside her desk. Tallinan's door was closed and locked. Good, she didn't like keeping her people late. Tired men made mistakes.

"All right Bundo, it's time to go. The escort should be waiting." They walked down the stairs and met up with O'Brien.

"All secure?" the Chief Petty Officer asked.

"Everything locked and checked," Cal replied. "I'm looking forward to an evening with a glass of brandy by the fire."

O'Brien pulled the door open. Men rushed into the Shed. They wore Navy uniforms, but none of them were men Cal recognized from her escort.

They carried clubs and swords. Bundo jumped at them, swinging the first thing that came to hand, a boat hook they used to hoist small items into the gondola.

"Get the Commander upstairs," Bundo shouted.

O'Brien pushed her up the stairs, staying between her and the attackers. The lead man ran up the stairs waving a club. O'Brien kicked him down the stairs, blocking the rest long enough for Cal to make the top. She ran along the hall. If she could get to the hatch, she could escape and bring reinforcements. A man stepped out of the shadows, a long knife in hand. O'Brien pulled her back of the man's reach and pushed her into her office. He slammed the door behind him. Cal picked herself off the floor in time to see Tallinan's arm come around O'Brien's neck. The point of his knife penetrated the front of O'Brien's uniform. The Chief Petty Officer collapsed soundlessly to the floor.

"I would love to stay and chat." Tallinan wiped his knife on O'Brien's shirt. "But I have a man to meet." He kicked Cal back against the wall. She lay gasping for air. "Weak, like this whole damn country." The man reached behind the bookshelf and pulled out the journal where Cal had been recording the changes she'd made in the plans. "My insurance." Tallinan hefted it. "I found it a while back and figured out what you'd been doing. Clever." He stuffed the plans from the desk in the back of his shirt. "Time to go." He threw papers into a pile then poured the contents of a flask on them. Lighting a match, he dropped it onto the papers which burst into flame.

Cal pushed herself up, but Tallinan went out the door. She heard banging on the other side and it didn't budge when she kicked at it. The room filled with smoke. She didn't have long. The window was her first thought, but she didn't think she'd survive the drop.

There was one possibility. It could be suicidal, but it was still better than burning alive. Cal snatched up her leather satchel, pulled the desk away from the wall, then kicked the panel to the hallway. She'd jammed it to keep it from opening accidentally. It took a second kick to open it. The flames behind her flared up as a draft blew in through the opening. Cal ran through it and kicked it shut behind her. Coughing in the smoke, Cal ran down the hall, pulled open the other door and ran up the stairs to the roof.

A shot rang out below her and a shadow ran across the Academy ground toward the gate. Tallinan.

Indistinct shouting came from the other end of the Shed where the main doors were. An explosion rocked the building, sending Cal to her knees. She ran to the storage barn on the roof and snatched up the Kite. It didn't take much time to assemble it and check it. Two more explosions shook the Shed, and flames broke through the roof not far away. Cal threw the harness she'd made around her, clipped herself to the wing and before she could doubt herself ran and threw herself off the roof.

The harness held her, letting her get her weight on the strap. She pushed her weight back and the nose of the wing came up and she glided in a wide curve. Landing too close to the Shed would put her in the hands of traitors. The shadow of Tallinan passed through the gate out into the city.

*Heat rises.* Cal swung back toward the Shed. The building had collapsed as she'd jumped. Now as she flew over it the hot air threw her high into the sky. Her clothes crisped in the heat, but she held her breath to keep her lungs safe. Once out of the direct heat Cal circled higher, then glided to where she'd last seen Tallinan. He ran down the street, stopping a couple of police officers and pointing back toward the Shed. One ran toward the fire, the other pulled out a whistle to blow, but fell when Tallinan punched him in the head. The Petty Officer kicked the downed man. Cal ground her teeth in rage. As Tallinan ran away down the street, Cal saw a coach waiting for him. It was dark, unmarked.

"No, you don't." She pulled her weight forward and swooped like a hawk, levelling out ten feet above the cobbles. The wind froze her as she rushed forward. Closer to the traitor now, she dropped further. At the last second, instead of passing over him, she threw her legs forward and unclipped herself from the Kite.

Her feet landed in the centre of his back and drove him face down into the cobbles. The Kite broke out of her grip and crashed into a building. Tallinan lay motionless on the cobbles. The coach moved toward her, but then the piercing sound of a police whistle split the night and booted footsteps approached from behind Cal and the coach rattled away into the night.

"Pardon me, Ma'am, but what is going on?"

"Treason and murder." Cal pointed at Tallinan. "Secure this man, leave the fire to the Navy."

Other whistles sounded and officers appeared a couple on horseback.

"I need your horse." Cal stopped one man and recognized the Inspector.

He jumped off. "Go."

"Inform the prince and move that thing out of sight." Cal pointed at the Kite. She shoved the journal into his hands. "Put this with it. Guard it with your life."

"Where are you going?"

"After a traitor." Cal leapt onto the horse and urged it into a gallop. She turned the corner and saw the coach ahead of her. This road was broad and the coachman had whipped the two horses into a flat run. Cal clung to her mount and prayed it didn't slip on the cobblestones. She knew this road; it led to the Kershian embassy. She couldn't let the coach make it there. Up ahead, she could already see where the road made a grand curve to approach the Embassy straight on. The coach would have to slow to make the curve.

Cal slowed her mount and swung to the left and followed a smaller road to another which ran straight past the gate. Setting her mount into a gallop again Cal raced toward the gate.

As soon as she was close enough to see the Anglian guards who stood outside the gate to the embassy, Cal shouted to them to stop the coach.

240

They finally heard and formed up on the road pointing their weapons toward the coach. One of them fired a shot and the sound of the coach changed as the driver hauled on the reins. Cal slowed and stopped her horse and jumped off, blessing the rides she'd taken in the mornings going to climb the wall.

"Commander Shillingsworth." she introduced herself to the honour guard. "The man in the coach has secret plans he intends to sell to the Kershians."

"She's the real thing," one of the guards shouted. "I climbed with her."

On the other side of the gate to the embassy, Kershian soldiers stood at alert with their own weapons.

Lord Sifton stepped out of the coach.

"I am on a delicate diplomatic mission. Let me pass."

"No, my Lord," the honour guard stood firm.

"She's the traitor," Sifton accused her. "She's been running about with the Kershian Ambassador. If you let her stop me, you will be harming the country."

"Sorry, my Lord." The ensign leading the honour guard stepped forward. "We have sent a message to the prince. Until he gets here, no one is entering the embassy."

"You there." Lord Sifton shouted to the Kershians. "Let me in. Now."

Bri strolled out of the embassy building to stand behind the Kershian guard. He spoke to them in his own language. They formed up across the gate, their weapons very deliberately not pointing at anyone on the Anglian side.

"Sorry, I have no authority on your side of the gate," Bri said smoothly. "For us to take any action would be tantamount to a declaration of war. I assure you, my Emperor would not be pleased."

Lord Sifton ranted, but when he turned to leave the guard refused to let him.

The royal coach rumbled up, and HRH Hubert climbed out.

"What have we here?"

"My Lord claims to be on a diplomatic mission."

"Does he?" the Prince looked at the now pale Lord Sifton. "I don't recall any diplomatic missions for tonight assigned to Lord Sifton. Or anyone else for that matter."

Sifton bolted toward the gate. The guards leapt to intercept him, but Sifton spun and dropped one guard with a punch to the neck and another with a kick to the gut. He leaped, caught the top of the gate and flipped over to the Kershian side.

"HOLD!" the prince bellowed. "Do not fire, no matter the provocation. He's on Kershian territory. I don't want to start a war over this waste of skin."

Lord Sifton sneered through the gate. "I know enough to bring Anglia to its knees."

"I very much doubt it." The prince waved his hand dismissively. "Clear this coach out of the way. Return to your posts." He walked up close to the gate. "My apologies for disturbing the peace of your embassy."

"No apology necessary." Bri bowed. "These things happen." He looked over to one of his soldiers. "Take the man into custody for now."

The soldier stepped over to Lord Sifton and took his arm. Sifton punched him in the gut and snatched up the rifle he dropped. He levelled the weapon at Cal.

The prince took a step toward her but was too far away. Sifton's face distorted with rage as he took up the slack on the trigger. The sound of two shots being fired rolled together so closely that they sounded almost like one.

Sifton span about. Bri stood behind him a pistol in his hand the smoke still lazily curling up and away from the barrel. He aimed one more time and sent a bullet through Sifton's heart.

"Well, that takes care of that." Bri returned his gun to his belt. "Please report to Her Majesty my determination that no shots were fired into Anglia from the Kershian side of the gate."

"I will do so." The prince bowed, the expression on his face curiously like admiration.

A man rode up at a gallop.

"Your Highness." He jumped off the horse and fell to his knees. "The Ferandican airship has broken loose of its mooring. Two men fell trying to restrain the craft. The wind is blowing it over the Channel."

"That is unfortunate. Send a Navy vessel to recover it."

"The princess, your daughter, is on it, with her son."

The Crown Prince went pale and for a horrible moment, Cal thought he'd faint.

"Your Highness, I need a ride in your coach." Cal stepped up to him. "You." She pointed to the guard who'd recognized her. "Secure Lord Sifton's coach. No one is to enter it for any reason. Keep it under heavy guard." She ran and climbed on the

Royal Coach followed by the prince. "We need to get to my house a fast as possible."

"Is there a way to rescue my daughter and grandson there?" The prince settled in beside her as they took off.

Call nodded absently, her mind hard at work. She looked up at the clouds. They were moving fast. From where the airship would have been moored, it could be over the water by now. She could make it to the princess if the envelope held. She willed the coach to go faster, but crashing would do no good either. When they pulled up to the house. Cal shouted for Hans and Bundo before remembering she didn't even know if he was still alive.

"I need your help, and your driver and guard too." Cal led them to the barn followed closely by Hans.

# Chapter 15  - First Flight

The Crown Prince stopped in the door and gasped. Cal turned back toward him. In different circumstances, she'd have laughed out loud at his expression.

"I did tell you I was making my own prototype from odds and ends." She pointed to the ropes holding the ship to the ground. "I'll need one of you on each of those. But first I need to untie the ropes from on top." Cal scrambled up a ladder on the wall and walked across the beams, untying the ropes from the airship. "Hans, put the shield in place under the heating unit. It will smother the fire and prevent sparks." She slid down the ladder and traded her uniform jacket for the thick leather one she wore to protect herself from sparks. She took the harness off and threw over a shoulder as she pulled the matching leather pants over the ones she wore. Simpler than needing to change. On impulse, she put on the cap, too, and hung her welding goggles around her neck.

The ship bobbed in the barn as Cal climbed into the gondola.

"Pass up the rope and some clips." She tossed the harness to the back out of the way, then used a boat hook to lift the coils of rope and bag of clips up to the gondola. "Pressure holding at 1500 psi. Good, open the roof, Hans."

"Open the roof?" The prince looked at her like she'd grown a second head. Hans pulled the levers to put the roof in motion.

"All right. Your Highness, I need you and your guard to stand by to loosen the ropes on the bow. Hans, you and the driver take the stern. You'll release on my mark. Pull the end until the knot opens then get out of the way. I don't know how quickly the ship will rise."

Wind curled in over the opening roof and pushed the ship about. Cal strapped in and put her hands on the valve to send steam to the engine. She wouldn't open the steering fins until she was well clear of the barn.

The roof thudded into place, leaving the barn open to the night sky.

"Pull the ropes on my mark. Three, two, one, mark."

The four men hauled on the mooring ropes, and the ship rocketed into the sky. The wind caught her and tossed her mercilessly about. Only the straps kept Cal from falling out of the craft. She cranked the wings open and locked the winch in place, then opened the valve to send power through the engine to the propeller.

The familiar howl sounded over the rush of wind and the prop hummed, pushing her ship against the wind. Cal hauled on the levers that controlled the angle of the fins. One up, one down. Her craft tilted crazily and spun until she levelled the wings.

Now that the airship flew with the wind the ride grew smoother, but cold air made her eyes water. Cal pulled the goggles up to protect her eyes and looked around. She had already risen much higher than the Kite had taken her. The wind told her the direction she needed to go.

Once the airship moved forward a slight downturn on the fins kept her from climbing higher. A wild guess about her speed told her it would be at least an hour before she caught up with the Ferandican airship.

Flying the airship reminded her of the exhilaration of sailing the Gates of Hell. It had the same intensity and demand for concentration. It had already been a long day, now it promised to be a long night.

The lights of the city winked out as she travelled farther and farther away. Soon after that, even the port lights faded from sight. From the air, the water of the channel was inky black. Tiny specks of light showed her where ships sailed the night.

Cold quickly became Cal's main concern. Even with her leather, she shivered as the wind blew past. She'd have to build a wood and glass unit on the next one, maybe capture heat from the steam to heat the gondola.

Cal's teeth chattered, but she watched ahead of her, looking for a shadow moving against the water. The cloud cover broke apart and a half moon helped with visibility. Just when she was about to despair, Cal spotted a shadow blowing through the air like paper across a street. The weight of the gondola kept the Ferandican ship from tumbling, but it spun ponderously in the air below her.

Cal pulled on a rope to let hydrogen escape from the envelope until flying with level fins kept her at the same altitude. Tilting them down again, Cal steered toward the larger ship.

The closer she got, the more worried Cal became. It would be a rough ride over there. She hoped the princess wasn't injured. The spinning would prevent any attempt at joining the ships. Cal thought of the Gates again.  Perhaps by heading into the wind, she could use her ship to stabilize the larger one, but she wouldn't have much time.

The ships approached each other. Cal got her ship as close as she dared, then locked down the steering levers. She undid the straps and crawled to the rear. Tying one end of the rope to a ring set in the keel, she fastened the other end to the boat hook in the centre. Next, she pulled on the harness, then tied the second harness, used clips to hold them together then fastened the harness to the rope. The second coil of rope went over her shoulder. Cal cut the back of the gondola open. She needed to keep the ships aligned.

Captain Henrichs had once spent an afternoon trying to teach Cal to throw the harpoon. They'd laughed a lot, but caught no fish. Now Cal stood in the gap, holding onto the gondola with her left hand, while she timed her throw for when a round window in the other gondola rushed toward her. The boat hook flew across the gap, smashing through the window. Cal dropped to the deck and held onto the ring with all her strength. The rope snapped tautly and hummed at such a high note she feared it would break. The forward pull of her ship slowly held the Ferandican airship steady.

Thanking whatever foresight had caused her to mount boiler and propeller below the gondola, Cal swung out onto the rope and slid across to the other ship. Her feet took up the momentum as she hit the gondola, and she hung from the rope against the hull of the airship. A clip in her hand made quick work of cleaning the remaining shards of glass from the window. Cal tied the end of the second rope to a clip on the first, then clipped it to herself, tying it off to give ten feet of leeway.

Cal gripped the frame of the window and unfastened her harness from the rope attaching the two ships.

"Princess!" Cal shouted as she pulled herself through the window. "Princess, can you hear me!?" Something moved over by the wall. Cal undid the short rope, fastened it to a nearby chair, then ran across the room. The woman looked younger than Cal. She huddled around a baby who, to Cal's relief fussed as soon as his mother moved. They were wrapped in several blankets against the cold.

"The crew fell attempting to stop the ship." The princess said through chattering teeth.

Cal took the baby and placed it on a blanket, then folded the cloth to make a bag. She lifted the princess to her feet and dragged her across the room. The short rope tied the blanket shut and made sure the child wouldn't fall if his mother lost her grip.

"Princess, pardon my familiarity." Cal hoisted up the woman's skirts and put the second harness on her, she clipped the two of them together, then fastened the princess to the rope.

"Hold your child. Keep your eyes closed. Pray if you want." Cal climbed out the window, hung from the harness as she hauled the princess and her baby through. All the climbing paid off as Cal hauled them hand over hand back to her airship. As she reached her gondola the vibration of the rope changed. Cal pulled herself up then yanked the princess in. They rolled across the floor as the rope snapped, leaving the near end flapping in the wind. They'd been far too close to death.

Cal squirmed out of her harness, then tied the princess to the ring.

"Sorry to abandon your ship, but I can't run it by myself and I don't think it could fly against the storm in any case. Hold on.

Back at the bow, Cal strapped in and unlocked the levers. The flight was rougher now as they flew against the wind. Each gust tossed them side to side. Whimpering behind her meant the princess lived. She had the blanket, but even then, she didn't have long at these temperatures.

The engine howled as Cal pushed the pressure to the limit of safety. The valve showed the pressure dropping, faster than she'd hoped. At this rate, they wouldn't make it safe to land. Not close, but closer than the land, lights shone against the black water. Cal steered toward the lights.

The lights belonged to a ship of the line. The watch shouted when they saw the airship. Cal held her position over the ship. A sailor climbed the loading crane. Sitting precariously balanced, he threw a rope up to her as she kept as close as she dared. Cal ran the rope around the rings holding Cal's straps to the main keel. She crawled to the back and pulled the princess and her child to the bow where she clipped the other woman to the rope, putting her leg through the loop of the empty harness, Cal lowered herself and the princess down the rope to the deck of the ship.

Sailor caught them and rushed them into the warmth of the infirmary. Cal wanted to tell them to cut the airship loose, but shaking overtook her and no words could make it past her chattering teeth. The ship's doctor plied them with warm sugar water and wrapped them in blankets with bed warmers.

Exhaustion pulled at Cal, but she refused to let sleep take her until the baby cried and the princess hushed at her son.

*** 

The HMSS Wellington steamed into port tugging the airship behind it, bobbing in the wind. The Captain informed Cal the crew had spent the night climbing up the rope and tying the airship down with the heaviest ropes they could manage. They didn't know what to do with the strange engine, so left it until the steam ran out.

Cal supervised the use of horses to pull the airship to where it could be securely moored in a sheltered place between two warehouses. The captain of the Wellington posted guards around it, then commandeered a steam carriage to take Cal, the princess and the infant to the palace in the city. A messenger had been dispatched as soon as they docked to inform the palace of the successful rescue.

"My father mentioned you in his letters." Princess Celia held Prince Tam gently, inspecting him at regular intervals as if to be sure he still breathed. "I had made my peace with God and determined to die bravely, keeping my son safe to the end. It still feels like a dream to be here, alive, warm and returning to the palace. I never imagined being rescued."

"Your father wanted Anglia to have its own airship. The one I flew is a prototype. I will have to design heating to make them useful."

"My husband's ship is cold, but we dress warmly and get heat from the boiler set in the centre of the ship. He will not be pleased to see your ship, which makes his look primitive. But I have never seen anything as beautiful."

"You are an ally, I'm sure we can help the prince improve his design."

"That too might anger him. He's a proud man."

As the steam carriage pulled into the palace grounds, HRH Hubert ran out to meet them, followed by Prince Stanagia of Ferandica at more dignified pace.

The Crown Prince hugged his daughter, unabashedly shedding tears. He ran a gentle finger across Tam's cheek.

"I am pleased to find you well." Prince Stanagia bowed over his wife's hand.

"My husband, I am pleased to be returned to your side." Princess Celia held Prince Tam up for her prince to see. "And your heir is safe and well."

The prince put his hand on his son's head as if in blessing. He walked over to Cal. "Commander Shillingsworth, I am forever in your debt." He bowed deeply. "My heart grieved at the loss of my family. It is as if you have restored them from death." In the depth of his eyes emotions flashed which put the lie to his formal tone.

"Your Highness." Cal bowed to him. "I am happy to serve you and the peace between our countries. I'm sure you, too, would have done the same."

Prince Stanagia smiled and for an instant, his cold face transformed into a brilliant joy before it vanished and she wondered if she'd imagined it.

"You honour me to assume such bravery of me." He swept another low bow, then took his princess' arm and walked with her back into the palace.

"I don't know what you said, but that's the most emotion I've ever seen from him." The Crown Prince offered her his arm, which made Cal suddenly aware she still wore her leathers, her goggles and cap hanging from her belt. She giggled as she put her hand on his arm and let him lead her into the palace.

***

Cal fought her body's desire for sleep. All day she'd been telling and retelling the story of the rescue. Princess Celia almost fainted when Cal talked about pulling her and Tam across the rope between the two ships.

"I am not fond of heights." She sipped at the brandy Prince Stanagia gave her. "But to please my husband I sail in his airship. To think of hanging by a thread so far above the ground." The princess went pale and sipped at her brandy. Prince Stanagia put his hand on hers. Her eyes widened, then she smiled at her husband.

"Personally, I am sure you are insane." The Crown Prince sipped at his tea. "I heard a report from a police officer who requested the Navy to recover a flying thing and a book. He said a woman came out of the sky like a hawk and drove a traitor to the ground. I didn't know you were working on something other than the airship."

"It was an early project which terrified me. However, when necessity forced me, it became a useful way to escape."

"Escape." HRH Hubert rolled his eyes and Cal had to restrain her giggles again. "Only you would plan to escape a burning building by leaping from the roof on a contraption of cloth and sticks." Then he frowned. "The fire will have set us back. My mother is not happy."

"Not as much as you might think, Your Highness. I expect to find a complete set of stolen plans in Lord Sifton's carriage. The journal returned to you holds the information I need to use the plans. All we need is a space to work and we can have a prototype ready for the spring."

"A space with a movable roof?"

"I would like to build such a place, but to do so now would slow us down. Anywhere sheltered from the worst of the wind will do for now."

"Movable roof?" Prince Stanagia looked over at Cal.

"If you wish, I can show you, but perhaps not today."

He nodded and whispered something in Princess Celia's ear. She smiled at him and he stood to offer his arm and escorted her from the room.

"The Prince is not a man given to showing his emotions. My daughter has been dutiful, but not always happy. What I've seen gives me hope she may find joy to match her duty."

"There is nothing like almost losing someone to give you perspective." Cal fought back a yawn. "Is there any news about Bundo and the others?"

"I haven't got a report yet from the Shed. Now, you are exhausted. I'm scared to guess when you last slept. My coach will take you to your home."

*** 

The driver escorted Cal to the door of her home. She walked in, climbed to her room, and fell into bed, waving at Beth on the way up the stairs. Sleep took her before her head hit the pillow.

Cal dreamed about the men in navy uniforms attacking. O'Brien dying with a knife in his back. She fought against the blankets. Noise from downstairs dragged her from slumber. The students must have finished some important exam to be causing such a row. She considered going to tell them to quiet down but decided not to spoil their fun. Cal closed her eyes and went back to sleep.

Hunger pangs woke her. Cal changed out of her leather and engineering clothes and put on a simple dress. She left her room then stopped at the top of the stairs. The stairs and hallway below looked like a battlefield. Red stains marred the parquet. The furniture lay in pieces; the walls were slashed with holes here and there. The rail on the stair had been broken, so Cal descended carefully and went to the dining room.

"Oh, you're awake." Beth smiled at her. "I'll get something for your breakfast."

"That would be nice." Cal sat in a chair and sighed. "What happened?"

"Not long after you went to sleep someone knocked on the door.  When I answered it, they pushed into the hall with four other men behind them. I screamed and tried to run. The students came out of the parlour and charged the men, who let me go. More ruffians come in through the back door. They tried to get up the stairs to where you were sleeping and those lovely people from the embassy stood on the stairs and didn't let one of them pass. The police came and hauled the men away, not that they had much work left to do after those students and the Zithayans were done."

"Anyone hurt?" Cal's hands shook, she didn't know whether from anger or shock.

"None of ours." Beth shrugged. "After the fight, Pentam and his family went to visit the Zithayan embassy. Crysabel was understandably shaken. They'll be leaving in a couple of weeks anyway now the boy has passed his dissertation and is officially Dr. Pentam Booksdale, Ph.D."

"So many people putting themselves in harm's way for my sake." Cal took a breath and tried to stop the shaking. "Bundo, McAllen, and it could have been you too."

"Haven't you heard about Bundo? One of the students said he was in the hospital."

"I must go see him."

"Not until after breakfast. After that, then Hans will take you."

The hospital smelled of blood and carbolic acid. A nurse guided Cal to the room where Bundo lay on a bed. Damp sheets covered his body and arms. At first, Cal feared him dead, but his chest moved.

"The cloth is for his burns," the nurse said. "I've never seen someone so burned and live. God willing, we will keep him alive, but his injuries are beyond us. Some people came from an embassy. They left herbs and ointments. The doctor is using them as it's more than what we'd have on our own."

"Pentam must have sent them." Cal leaned over Bundo. "Hold fast, my warrior." She went from there to the Zithayan Embassy where she asked for Hyansea at the gate. The guards waved her through. She met her friend in the hall. Hyansea led her to a room where Pentam and Crysabel sat with the twins. They were practicing their Zithayan, voices not as musical as the native speakers, but they didn't stumble over words.

"This one must apologize." Hyansea bowed to Cal. "The people we sent to your home were more than we said they were."

"I heard they repelled an attack on the second floor of my home."

"Nyian and La are skilled warriors. We heard rumours and knew your home was being watched. We wished to keep our friends safe."

Cal stood and bowed low.

"This one is in debt for your kindness. Your warriors kept my friends safe."

"Sadly, your home was damaged."

"Wood and brick can be repaired."

"This one has heard you have influence with Her Majesty."

"Not a lot, to be honest."

"Would you be willing to carry a missive on our behalf and encourage her to consider its contents?"

"I will carry your message."

Hyansea took a scroll from her sleeve and handed it to Cal.

"If you are able, place this in the hands of one who stands by your Queen."

Cal tucked the scroll away and shared tea with Hyansea, Pentam and Crysabel, entertaining them with her attempts at Zithayan.

# Chapter 16  - New Command

A month after the rescue, the royal coach came to collect Cal. She wore a gown Beth helped her put on. None of her uniform clothing was in a fit state to visit royalty. Cal touched the Zithayan's scroll in her sleeve. She'd ask the prince for advice.

An honour guard met her at the entry to the palace and marched with her to a large room with the Queen seated on a dais at the end. The Crown Prince sat beside her.

The guards walked Cal close to Her Majesty. When they stopped, Cal went to her knee.

"How may I serve, Your Majesty?"

"Our son has told me of your adventures. A flying ship, a mid-air rescue, fire and treachery. If it weren't him, We would wonder if it was the plot of a penny dreadful."

"It has been a busy time." Cal studiously kept her eyes on the floor in front of her.

Her Majesty laughed and a murmur went through the room making Cal aware a crowd surrounded her.

"Is there something you wish of Us in return for your service?"

"Your Majesty, I am your subject. I need no reward for fulfilling my duty," Cal took a breath. "However, friends came to my aid and I owe them a debt. They asked I deliver this message and ask you to consider its contents." Cal held the scroll in her hand. A page came and took the scroll from her hand and passed it to Her Majesty. The queen opened it, glanced at it and passed it to the Crown Prince.

"We will speak of this later. Please rise." The Queen gazed at Cal. "Our son granted you the equivalent of a knighthood, Lady Shillingsworth. We are told he neglected to make any ceremony to mark the occasion. It is a habit which We are trying to break. In this case, We do not agree with his assessment. Your actions have shown you to be deserving of much greater honour than a knighthood conferred in a field with no one to witness." She put out her hand and the Crown Prince drew his sword and handed it over.

"Calliope Shillingsworth, Commander of the Royal Engineers, come forward and kneel in front of Us."

Cal walked up the two steps to the dais, where the prince helped her to kneel in the gown.

The steel flashed in the corner of Cal's eyes, on one side then the other, striking her shoulders with a feather touch.

"Lady Calliope, We confer on you the knighthood of the realm. Further, We name you Marquise Shillingsworth. Lord Sifton's estates and holding are forfeit to the Crown. Not wishing to burden you with the care of his dependents, We confer the equivalent land and holdings from the Crown to be an income for you and your descendants."

Cal gasped in shock.

"There is one last issue We must address. You are commissioned as the Commander of the Royal Engineers, a rank equivalent to Admiral in our Navy. It is Our desire for you to find and train a replacement for your commission. It is Our decision that you will serve this land better as the Admiral of the Anglian Royal Air Navy. Land has been set aside for you to construct what you need to build the fleet We intend you to command. Rise, Marquise Shillingsworth, Admiral of the First Fleet of the Royal Air Navy."

Cal stood with the Prince's aid. He handed her a scroll.

"This is a list of your holdings. I will have a man you the extent of your estate and confer with you on how you may wish to run it." Next, he showed her a pin made of gold and diamond. It showed a gear with a crown above it, and on either side of the gear exquisitely carved gold wings lifted. "The sign of your rank. The palace will instruct your tailor on what we wish you to wear as your uniform." He pinned it on her gown. "My son-in-law, the Prince of Ferandica, has asked to honour you on his country's behalf."

Prince Stanagia stepped forward and bowed to Cal.

"Marquis Shillingsworth, Ferandica owes you deep thanks for your courage and determination. My heart has been mended by your actions. I grant you exclusive use of my royal villa. Treat it as your own. I also name you as a friend of Ferandica. You will always be welcome in our country, and you may call on any of our embassies for aid in any matter. Though you have no title or rank in Ferandica, you are granted access to the ear of the King." The Prince took a soft bag from his pocket and dropped a ring into the palm of his hand. "Wear this ring as a sign of our friendship." He passed it to Cal, who slid it onto the ring finger of her right hand. It was a simple gold band holding a ruby carved with a crest.

"Your Highness, it will be my pleasure to visit your country when duty permits." She curtsied.

The prince kissed her hand. Then the Crown Prince turned her to face the room.

"Welcome the newest peer of the realm."

***

"Our late husband had a fondness for brandy We could never understand." The Queen passed Cal a snifter from a tray held by a servant. Cal took her time to appreciate the drink. Her Majesty sipped at her tea and waited patiently.

"As expected, your late husband had very good taste." Cal let the drink slide like silk down her throat. She'd never imagined anything like it.

"Are you aware of the contents of the scroll you delivered?" The Crown Prince sipped at his own glass of brandy.

"No, Your Highness."

"The Zithayan Dynasty wishes to open talks with Anglia and Ferandica in response to what they see as an inevitable war with the Kershian Empire. They suggest we send a diplomat along with Dr. Booksdale and his wife. We are planning to do so.

Even the chance to speak with the Zithayans is an opportunity not to be wasted.

"Speaking of diplomacy, the wreckage of the Ferandican airship has been recovered. The Crown is asking the Royal Engineers to help in the rebuilding of the ship. Not with the newest boiler and engine, but with enough improvement to allow Our daughter to fly with more confidence."

"We would be delighted. I will split the group between setting up to build the prototype and repair of the Ferandican airship."

"Perhaps you can come up with a way to return your ship to the City and your workshop. It is too valuable to be moored between warehouses."

"I will need a heavy wagon, but it is doable. Once the pressure is up, it is only a matter of waiting for good weather."

***

Cal and Hans drove the wagon with the furnace for the airship to the port. She put the guards and winches she'd brought to work pulling the ship into position over the furnace. The guards took turns pumping the tank to fill the line with water. Hans lit the fire and they left the guards to watch the pressure gauge.

"Move this lever to cut the fire when the pressure reaches 1500psi. Don't worry about putting the fire out, the shield will block most of the heat."

"Hope I'm here to see the Impossible fly," one of the guards said.

"The Impossible?" Cal's lips twitched.

"Sorry, Ma'am. It's what we called it after you appeared out of the night. Scared us right proper, but the Captain's thinking about what to do for the next time."

"Is he now?" Cal looked toward the harbour. "Maybe I should pay him a visit."

The visit turned into a full-blown formal inspection with Cal being piped on board, even without her being in uniform. The first mate gave her a full tour of the ship. It was Cal's first chance to see a ship of the line. The Kestrel would look like a dingy next to the Wellington. The crew watched her out of the corners of their eyes, straightening in pride that it was their ship she'd landed on.

"I'm honoured you stopped by." Captain Hennass passed her a glass of brandy. "I got word you were bringing equipment down for the airship but didn't expect to see you here."

"The crew apparently has named her 'The Impossible'." Cal grinned. "It's not a bad name. Perhaps someone could paint it on the gondola. I'm already planning to rebuild it, but the name will stay."

"I will see it gets done."

"One of the guards mentioned you were thinking about ways to make the next time easier. What ideas have you come up with?"

"We'll need a winch, a clear space on the deck so she doesn't dangle at the end of the rope. In any kind of weather, it would be dangerous. Cleats to tie down to, of course."

"Sounds like you have things well in hand." Cal sipped at her drink. "I'd suggest at least two winches. I'm going to put in a pulley system to make it easier to lift things in and out of The Impossible. I hadn't thought of adding mobile support for the airships, but if we are going to travel great distances it will be essential. How would you feel about being transferred to a support role in the Royal Air Navy?"

"If the Admiralty approves, the crew and I would be honoured." Captain Henass stood and saluted.

"Keep it to yourself for the moment, but I will give it serious thought. I expect the Wellington may get a major overhaul if we go forward with it."

"My orders keep us in domestic waters, so we'll be handy to the shipyard."

"I will see it stays that way until I know for sure."

"Very good, Commander."

Cal finished her drink, then was escorted from the ship to where Hans waited with a cab to take them to the train station.

"Leaving the furnace on the wagon was good thinking." Hans looked out the window. "We'll build another one for the barn. That will make it easier to get her home."

"I'm thinking of retrofitting the Wellington as a support vessel for the Air Navy. Same idea as the wagon but even more so. She can carry parts and do repairs without bringing the airship home. Gives The Impossible more range. And soon her sister ships as well."

"Her Majesty's Airship, The Impossible..." Hans rubbed his chin. "Has a nice ring to it."

***

"Your Highness, the trip on The Impossible will be at least cold and uncomfortable, at worst it is dangerous." Cal glared at the Crown Prince.

"I'm riding back with you." He didn't blink, and Cal sighed.

"Very well. You will need the warmest clothes you can find, and a pair of goggles to protect your eyes from the wind. We leave at daybreak for the port the first day which has good enough weather for the trip. I will send a messenger to the palace."

Three days later she sat beside the Crown Prince in the royal car on the way to the port by train. They had hot tea and breakfast laid out. Cal had replaced her leather work jacket with one lined with sheepskin. The prince had a similar coat flung over the back of a chair.

At The Impossible, Cal double-checked the boiler pressure and fastened ropes to the rings at either end of the keel. She then coiled and fastened them to the floor of the gondola. The prince tied himself to the ring at the rear while Cal strapped in.

"Stand by to release mooring ropes." Cal cranked the fins out into position. The slight breeze tossed them about. "Release."

The Impossible floated up and clear of the warehouses. She hadn't topped up the hydrogen, so their buoyancy was closer to neutral. Better for flying, anyway.

Cal fed power to the engine and The Impossible headed across the port as she rose higher into the air.

"That should be good." Cal levelled the fins after turning to follow the railway track back to the city. "I'll need a better way to steer. Don't want to lose any passengers when we turn. Maybe something driven by foot pedals."

"You're the engineer." The prince sat watching out the back of the Gondola. "I never imagined this."

"Quite something isn't it?" Cal said. "I didn't have much chance to enjoy the first trip. It was too dark to see much."

The noise of the engine and propeller made conversation a challenge. The prince didn't look interested in talking anyway.

When they reached the city, Cal left the tracks and looking down, tried to figure where they were in relation to her home. She saw the river in the distance and the bridge where they'd been attacked. Now she knew where they were, so she steered toward homewards.

Hans had the roof open, Navy personnel standing by to assist. Cal flew over the barn and lowered the power until they hung high over her home.

"Drop the rope out the stern, Your Highness." Cal pushed the bow rope out.  "I will release hydrogen to drop slowly."

The Impossible drifted down. Cal felt the shift through the floor when the ropes were fastened to the winches and they started pulling the airship down into her berth. She cut the power to the engine and stopped the hydrogen release. Twenty minutes later, The Impossible floated in the barn as the roof slowly closed above it. Cal lowered the rope ladder and suggested the Prince climb down first. Cal inspected her craft, then gave it a pat before following him down.

"A pleasure flying with you." The Prince saluted and Cal returned it. "Mother is looking forward to the experience."

"Her trip will be much more comfortable."

Cal set the guards to maintain watch outside the barn.

"It is too much to hope our arrival wasn't noted." Cal pointed at the ship. "It was somewhat dramatic after all. You are ordered to destroy the ship if you are put in a position where you can't defend it. I fully expect airships will appear in other countries, but there is no reason we need to make it easy on them. Your Highness, if you would honour me and join me for tea? Beth has been cooking up a storm in the hopes you would stay for a visit."

"I would be delighted, Marquise."

***

Three days later, the coach from the Zithayan Embassy stopped by to allow Pentam and Crysabel to say farewell before they started on their journey toward the Dynasty.

"I am going to miss you." Cal brushed her finger across Calli's cheek.

"What about me?" Pentam grinned at her.

"Certainly, but there is something about holding Calli which pushes all the worries away."

"I know what you mean." Pentam looked over at Crysabel holding Andrew. The love in his eyes made Cal sigh inwardly. They were so lucky.

"We will write at every opportunity," Crysabel said. "Hyansea says it will be months before we get there, even with taking the train across Locania to Hassarah. It will mean we don't need to sail around the whole continent. We'll board ship in Sombi. The University is on the far side of the Dynasty, so not many outsiders have ever been there."

"I will look forward to hearing of your adventures." Cal tried to smile. "I'm glad Hyansea is accompanying you, but I'll miss her visits."

Her friends climbed into the coach and waved one last time

"You are kind, Cal. I have left a note introducing you to my successor. Please consider showing her the hospitality you have given me."

"Of course."

Hyansea climbed into the coach as Crysabel shut the window. The driver snapped the reins and they were off.

"I understand you wish a tour of your estate, Marquise?" A man climbed out of a waiting coach. "I'm Fredrick Gooly. His Highness has given me a list."

"Yes, I need something to distract me, or I'll spend the day moping about." Cal climbed into the coach. "Shall we go?"

They made several stops. The first was at a large mansion on the far side of the river.

"This has been held by the Crown for the better part of a decade. It's been used to house guests, but recently has remained empty most of the time." Frederick climbed out of the coach. "The staff will show you through the house.

The place was at least three times the size of her home.

"What am I going to do with this much space?"

"That is up to you, Marquise." Frederick waited as the coachman helped Cal in, then followed. "The Crown has given you the estate complete, so you may use it for whatever you like, even sell it. Though I wouldn't recommend it, you wouldn't get a good price."

"So I could set up offices there."

"If you wish. The Navy will provide offices for your work with them," he pointed out.

"I was thinking more along the lines of a Society of Engineers." Cal glanced back at the house.

"There is no formal training for engineers, perhaps it is time. If I'm to train the new Commander of the Royal Engineers, we will need a steady supply of talented people."

"It would be an interesting project," Frederick said. "Now the next stop is at a suite of rooms a family used when they visited the city. They reverted to the Crown when the family ended without an heir."

By the end of the day, Cal had seen most of the city, and viewed houses, rooms and warehouses all in an immaculate state and kept by a minimum staff.

"Your country estate is too far away to visit today. It is near the main railway running south, a half a day's trip. When you wish to inspect it, I will make arrangements. It is more useful in the summer in any case."

"Country estate?" Cal rubbed her temples.

"Of course."

"I would like a listing of the staff at each location, what they are being paid. Can I hire them, or must I find my own people?"

"I am sure the Crown would be willing to let you hire some of the staff. Others have positions which will make it difficult to let them go."

"So the first person I need will be someone to manage the staff and paying them."

"That would be a good plan. I can recommend a couple of people if you wish."

"Great. Send their names to me at my home and I'll take it from there."

The coach pulled up in front of Cal's home.

"One last piece of advice, Marquise," Frederick leaned back as the coachman opened the door. "If you wish to create a society, you may want to apply for a royal warrant."

"Excellent idea," Cal climbed out of the coach. "I will speak to the prince about it."

***

The Royal Engineers gathered in a warehouse near the edge of the city, not far from the field where Cal had first seen the Ferandican airship.

"We will have a functioning airship by spring." Cal looked at the group, now numbering over a hundred men. "For the winter we will be manufacturing the pieces of the ship here and in other warehouses in the area. They will be assembled later in a different location."

"I heard an airship flew over the city, not much more than a week ago," Landers said.

"That was The Impossible, my personal airship."

"Personal airship?" Landers widened his eyes. "I'm guessing that is how you achieved the rescue everyone is talking about but knows nothing for sure."

"Correct." Cal swept her gaze across her team. "As part of the design work, I will be taking each of you up in her as weather permits. I expect you to make detailed notes of areas of improvement."

"What about that?" Ensign Cesare pointed to the Kite leaning against the wall in the corner.

"We will get to it in time," Cal said. "Right now I need you to determine what you need to make this a functioning airship factory. This warehouse will be for metal fabrication and construction. The one next door will handle the wood framing and gondola. Another behind us will be where we put the envelope together. I want reports on my desk by the end of the week."

"Is it true you're leaving?" Engineer Second Class Patrick asked.

"Yes, but not right away. I will be commanding the Air Navy, but until I have a Navy to command, you'll have to put up with me."

***

Cal sat alone listening to the concert. Frederick hadn't taken her to see the private box, but it was listed on her estate. Some evenings she brought guests, engineers or students. The work in the factories had started as Christmas approached, but Cal felt restless. The music helped calm her so she could think clearly. Tonight, she didn't want company. Crysabel's recent letter full of excitement made Cal depressed. She wanted more than sitting in an office giving orders.

"Marquise Shillingsworth." Bri slipped into the box and sat behind her, out of sight of anyone in the hall.

"Cal to my friends."

"Cal." Bri sighed. "I'm not sure I should have that honour. War is coming. I love my country, but I don't love the direction it is heading. I will be returning home, shortly. The failure of certain people in the embassy has been placed on my shoulders. I know your response, but I find I cannot leave without asking, however foolish it may be."

Cal's heart thumped.

"Ask then." She didn't turn around.

"I would like to introduce you to my daughter, show you the beauty of Kershia." Bri stopped so long Cal wondered if he'd left. "Would you consider coming home with me?"

"Would you stay here?"

"I can't." Bri's voice was pained. It made Cal think of his eyes the last time they'd met at a concert.

"You know my answer." Cal closed her eyes. "I wish for a day when I can visit your home as a friend."

"Our countries will be at war, if not in the coming year, then in the next. We will be enemies..." Bri growled at her.

"Until you act as an enemy, I will count you as a friend."

"You honour me more than you should." The chair creaked as Bri stood. "Farewell, Cal. Be careful, there are people who wish you harm."

"I will always have enemies," Cal said, but she didn't think he heard her.

The orchestra returned to the stage and played the next piece on the program. Cal wiped at the corners of her eyes and then let the music, like her airship, carry her away.

Alex McGilvery

# Acknowledgements

This is the second in the Calliope Series. She introduced herself in Calliope and the Sea Serpent, then informed me she expected a series of her own.

Lea Carter, Naomi P. Cohen beta read for me and gave me great feedback. Chris Lum did the copy-edit. He's a new copy editor for me, but did a fantastic job, very focused on details. chrislumcopy.wordpress.com

A.P. Fuchs did the cover again another eye-catching design.

I was fortunate to find the airship on the cover made by Paul Potiki, at www.bookcoverwhisperer.net

# **About the Author**

Alex is an author, editor and reviewer living in Kamloops, B.C. He has two dogs who drag him out for walks, and a scotch collection to celebrate the successful completion of his next goal. Living with his son and grandchildren has created a new source of plot material.

# Other books by Alex

**Spruce Bay Books:**
Wendigo Whispers
Cry of the White Moose
**The Belandria Tarot**
The Devil Reversed
The Regent's Reign

Generation Gap
The Gods Above
Tales of Light and Dark
Like Mushrooms (poetry and photography)
The Heronmaster
Blood and Sparkles, and other stories
Princess of Boring
By the Book
Sarcasm is My Superpower
Playing on Yggdrasil
The Unenchanted Princess
**Alex also has stories in:**
Shards (releasing in November 2018)
Slave to the Axe Song
Canadian Creatures
Words on the Rocks
Beyond the Wail
Collidor Stream Collection 2016

Read short stories and excerpts from his
novels at alexmcgilvery.com

9 781989 092088